Mystery of the Haunted Mine

By **GORDON D. SHIRREFFS**

(Original Title: *The Haunted Treasure of the Espectros*)

Cover by Dom Lupo

Published by Scholastic Book Services, a division of Scholastic Magazines, Inc., New York, N. Y.

Dedicated to my only daughter

CAROLE ALICE SHIRREFFS

in the hope that some day she will
find a lost treasure, not necessarily
a material one

Single copy price 45¢.
Quantity prices available on request.

 This Scholastic Book Services edition is published by arrangement with Chilton Books.

3rd printing..March 1966

Printed in the U.S.A.

CONTENTS

1 The Lure of the Lost Espectro Mine

THE ESPECTRO MOUNTAINS rose almost impetuously from the desert floor to loom high over the scattered ranches along the southern and western bases of the mountains. The Espectros dominated that lonely part of Arizona as nothing else did. They stood proudly and mysteriously against the blue, cloud-dotted sky of day and loomed dark and brooding at night. They could be seen for many miles in all directions and had been used by travelers as the one outstanding landmark in that isolated land, for the other mountains in the hazy distance were as nothing when compared to the

Espectros. They could be seen long before travelers could distinguish any particular features of the great jumbled masses of rock that formed them. When one was near them they seemed almost to lean over, as though to overpower insignificant humans with their ponderous might. Even when one was miles beyond the Espectros, it was difficult not to obey a compelling impulse to turn and look back at them. They had the uncanny power of making people look at them again and again and yet never tire of the view. Still there was a hidden seed of fear that sprouted rapidly within those who looked at them for too long a time. Their very name, given to them by the early Spanish explorers, was an indication of the fear and respect which the brooding mountains had always seemed to instill in those who studied them. The Espectro Mountains—the Ghost Mountains! For they *were* haunted, as surely as the fears of man could people such places with the ever-restless spirits of the dead.

Gary Cole unsaddled his claybank and placed the saddle on top of the corral rail. His eyes sought the Espectros. He well knew the aura of thralldom, mingled with intense fear and curiosity, that hung over the Espectros like the heat haze of these late summer days. All of his life had been spent within view of the Espectros. The night of his birth the Thunder People had thudded their drums in the rain-streaming canyons of the mountains and had shot their lightning arrows through the dark skies to bathe the Espectros in an eerie bluish light. An old Chiricahua *vaquero* who was working on the ranch at that time had prophesied that Gary would be held in subjection to the Espectros no matter where he roamed, and that he always would be compelled to come back to them.

Gary leaned on the rail and shoved back his hat. The Espectros were clothed in a smoky-looking haze which distorted and magnified them. It had been a busy summer for Gary, and in two weeks he would be back in high school without having had the chance to explore the Espectros thoroughly. It had been a summer of hard work with little time to play, and the money he had made was not his to keep. It was sorely needed in the Cole household, for Chiricahua Springs Ranch was no longer a paying proposition since Gary's father had become an invalid.

He watched a puff of cloud chase its fleeting shadow down the rugged slopes of the Espectros in a race that would never end. He saw a still-winged hawk hanging almost motionless high over

The Needle like a scrap of charred paper pasted against the startling blue of the sky. The naked pinnacle of rock known as The Needle thrust itself up from the harsh slope of a great peak like a warning finger to those who would probe into the secrets of the Espectros. But for those who *did* venture into the mountains, The Needle was always the starting point. For not only were those mysterious mountains haunted by strange and bloody tales handed down by Apaches, Spaniards, and Americans, but also by the persistent whispered rumors of vast stores of gold and silver left locked within the bosom of the mountains by the legendary Melgosa Brothers, over a hundred years ago.

Gary half closed his eyes. It was almost four o'clock. He looked directly at the sheer rock wall to the right of, and just beyond, the towering finger of The Needle, now fully lighted by the dying sun. Just then Gary heard the old pendulum clock in the Cole living room strike the hour. As the last stroke died away he opened his eyes to stare at the rock wall in the canyon. For a fleeting instant he thought he saw something like a line cut into the rock, but he couldn't be sure whether it was natural or not. Then it was gone as quickly as it had appeared, leaving him with a bitter feeling of disappointment. Swiftly the rock wall became shrouded in shadow until the entire canyon was dark and uninviting.

He turned quickly to walk to the house, and as he did so he saw his father, leaning on his crutches, staring toward the same canyon. Gary turned away; he didn't want to embarrass his father. He picked up his little Winchester saddle gun from its position against the corral rail. It needed a cleaning, for he had killed a rattler that day. Gary had been guiding dudes from a local ranch, and when the rattler had struck savagely at the horse of one of the dudes, Gary had killed it with a shot through the ugly flat head. Now there was a five-dollar bill folded in his shirt pocket—a grateful gift from the sweating dude. Gary had not told him it was the only cartridge in his rifle.

"Gary!" called his mother from the kitchen.

"Yes, Mother?"

"Wash up. We're eating early tonight. Your father and I are going into The Wells tonight to stay with Aunt Marion. Do you want to come with us?"

Gary, a year before that time, would have been only too happy to go to Cottonwood Wells, but he had been a kid then. It just wasn't right for a guy *his* age to be seen riding into The Wells with his father and mother, no matter how much he loved them.

"Gary?" questioned his mother.

"Well, I was figuring on studying my maps and things, Mother."

"You know them by heart, Gary."

He filled a basin with water, washed quickly, and combed his thick reddish hair. When he walked into the pleasant-smelling kitchen his mother turned to look at him, brushing back a lock of her own thick titian hair. It was a beautiful red against the blue of her eyes and the fairness of her skin. Lucille Hart had been the belle of Cottonwood Wells before she had married Pete Cole just before Pearl Harbor when he was a sergeant in the Marines. Pete Cole had brought home a fine war record, plus a Navy Cross and a piece of steel lodged near his spine which had partially crippled him. A strange event in a branch of Cholla Canyon had crippled him still further and had almost cost him his life.

Gary eyed his pretty mother as he set the table for her. There were dark circles beneath her lovely blue eyes and every day new worry lines appeared on her forehead. "I was hoping you'd go with us this time, Gary," she said a little petulantly. She didn't quite realize her only child was swiftly growing into a man.

Pete Cole came into the kitchen, slid into his chair, and leaned his crutches against the wall. "I'd rather have Gary stay here," he said. "Jim Kermit said he had seen a mountain lion prowling about the wash just east of the ranch. I think Gary had better stay here and keep an eye on the stock, Lucille."

"The *stock*, Pete?" questioned Lucille. "There's hardly enough to bother with. Now I think . . ." her voice broke off as she saw the taut look on his face. Pete Cole still liked to *think* he was a rancher.

Gary busied himself with his food. His father knew well enough why Gary didn't want to go to The Wells with them. It was hardly likely a cougar would be seen around there in the summer, and during daylight hours at that.

"All right, Pete," said Mrs. Cole. She had been through this before. Men always seemed to stick together, even the two she loved and cherished above everything else.

"You're off tomorrow, eh?" asked Gary's father.

"It's Sunday, Dad," said Gary.

Pete Cole fiddled with his knife. "What are you planning to do?"

There was no sense in lying, and besides it wasn't easy to lie to his father. Gary had learned that at an early age. "I thought I'd ride up past The Needle," he said.

"Looking for more relics?"

"Yes."

"And maybe a lead to the Lost Espectro, eh, Gary?"

Gary flushed. "I didn't think there would be any harm in that."

"I've told you quite a few times this summer to forget about the Lost Espectro."

"It isn't easy, living right in the shadow of the Espectros, to forget about the treasure hidden up there." Gary leaned forward. "The Lost Espectro is supposed to be richer than the Dutchman's Lost Mine, the Lost Adams Diggings, the Lost Padre, and maybe Tayopa itself!"

"Fairy tales! Lies embroidered by old-timers!"

"The Dutchman brought out gold from the Superstitions, didn't he? Adams found a bonanza and researchers agree that perhaps others found it as well and lost it again! The Lost Padre exists! You told me yourself you used to hunt for it on weekends when you went to college in El Paso. You just can't deny Tayopa, Dad. The old records in Mexico prove that Tayopa was one of the richest silver mines in the world!"

"Take it easy," said Mrs. Cole nervously. She glanced at her husband.

But Gary was warming up to his favorite subject. It was almost an obsession with him. "My great-grandfather spent a large part of his later life looking for the Lost Espectro," Gary continued, "and actually made a *derrotero* of his findings! He told your father the chart was as accurate as he could make it. He said that on his deathbed. Would he lie to his own son when he was dying? You yourself have always said that Great-grandfather Cole's *derrotero* probably held the key to the Lost Espectro if anything did!"

"Maybe it does, son," said Pete Cole quietly, "but where is it?"

This last remark was like a dash of cold water against Gary's face. The chart, or *derrotero,* had vanished years ago.

"I saw you looking for that legendary Spanish miner's symbol that is supposed to be cut into the east wall of The Needle Canyon, Gary. I know it's supposed to be visible about four o'clock in the afternoon during the late part of the summer. Did you happen to see it today?"

Gary couldn't help himself. "Did *you,* Dad?"

It was Pete Cole's turn to flush. He glanced quickly at his wife.

Lucille Cole stood up and began to clear the table. "Yes, Pete," she said quietly, "Gary knows you still look for it. How can you expect him to forget about the Lost Espectro when you haven't forgotten about it yourself?"

"There's nothing but death up there for those who look for it," said Pete.

"Yet *you* searched for it, Pete."

"Are you siding with Gary?" he snapped.

"No, Pete. But he's as like you as you were like your grandfather. Your own father was a rancher, and he never thought about the Lost Espectro."

"I consider myself a rancher, Lucille!"

She smiled. "By birth rather than by choice I think, Pete. I can remember when we were in high school in Cottonwood Wells how the other girls used to talk about you. But you were always more interested in lost treasures than you ever were in girls."

"Until I got interested in you, Lucille," he said.

"But you were still looking for the Lost Espectro even after you came back from the war, Pete."

He looked down at his almost useless legs. "For a time," he said bitterly.

Gary began to help his mother. It hadn't been so many years ago that Pete Cole had been fired upon by a hidden marksman while he was searching an offshoot of Cholla Canyon for clues to the Lost Espectro. His horse had been shot to death and in the fall Pete had suffered damage to his spine, which had already been injured by his war wound. He had been found by Jim Kermit, a local rancher, a full day after his fall. His condition now prevented him from ever again riding into the Espectros.

Pete Cole got to his feet and reached for his crutches. "Gary," he said sternly, "I don't want you ever to ride past The Needle. That's final!" He dragged himself from the kitchen.

Gary looked at his mother. "I'll do the dishes," he said.

"He means it, Gary."

"I won't go beyond The Needle," he promised. He smiled ruefully. "Not much reason to, I guess. I haven't found any leads to the Lost Espectro."

She took off her apron. "Tuck called," she said.

"I'll call him right back," Gary said eagerly.

"No need to. I told him to come out and stay with you tonight."

He stared at her. "But you asked me to go to The Wells with you and Dad tonight."

She kissed him. "I don't need a lost *derrotero* to tell me the obvious," she said. "Remember, Gary! Do not go past The Needle!"

He watched her as she walked toward the door into the living room. She seemed so tired. "Mother," he called out. She turned and looked at him questioningly. He reached into his shirt pocket and took out the folded five-dollar bill. He handed it to her. "Buy a hot dog and a bottle of soda pop for yourself and Dad," he said.

She eyed the money and then her big son. "Where did you get this?"

"The Lost Espectro," he said. He swung out his arms. "The place was loaded with bales of 'em, but I wasn't greedy."

She reached out and touched his forehead. "Gold fever," she said quietly.

Later, after his father and mother had left in the battered green pickup truck, Gary walked outside and looked at the dusky light over the mountains. For thirty years persistent stories had lingered about mysterious murders and disappearances in the Espectros. Rifle shots from the clinging, dark shadows of canyons had turned back seekers of the lost treasure supposedly hidden in the mountains. Skeletons had been found in remote, sun-drenched canyons with bullet holes in the grinning skulls. Men had entered those brooding mountains and had never been seen again.

Purple shadows now filled the canyons and hollows. Only the highest peaks of the Espectros were still bathed in the intermingled rose and gold wash of the last rays of the dying sun. The mountains looked so quiet and still, so peaceful and pleasant; and yet, mysterious death waited up there, haunting the silent canyons and the lonely purple mesas, as it had haunted them for many years.

Then the sun was gone from the upper tips of the peaks as though a master hand had flicked a switch. A cold wind began to search through the canyons and to whisper down the darkened slopes. Far across the silent desert came the drifting, melancholy crying of a coyote. Gary shivered a little. The windmill ground into slow life and the whirring blades sang a sad little song of their own. It was then that something seemed to catch at the corner of Gary's left eye—a pinpoint of yellow light, quickly coming and vanishing high on the rugged slopes beyond the looming pinnacle of The Needle.

Gary narrowed his eyes. No one lived up there. The local Apaches, with cold horror, shunned the thought of entering those mountains after dark.

The ranchers entered the fringe canyons of the Espectros only during daylight, always armed and never alone. Those few men who were caught in there after dark never showed a light.

It had always seemed to Gary that the mountains moved in closer at night like a huge crouching beast, a beast that stared at the lonely Cole Ranch, slowly licking its thick wet lips, baring every now and then a long yellow fang, poisonous and sharp as a needle. Some dark night . . .

Cold green fear flowed through Gary. He glanced quickly at his rifle which leaned against the wall of the house. "Lobo!" he called sharply. There was no answer from the huge dog. In fact Gary had not seen him all that day.

Gary walked to the low sprawling house that had been built near Chiricahua Springs in 1866 by his great-grandfather, a tough and hardened veteran of the Civil War. James Cole had fought Apaches and squatters to hold his land. Bullet holes and arrow nicks pocked the thick adobe walls. Beyond the ranch buildings, closer to the ever-flowing springs, was the private cemetery of the Coles'. Gary's great-grandmother lay buried there, with three Apache bullet holes in her. There were others there who had died violently, some of them by the hand of Jim Cole himself. It was a hard country. It was peaceable now, but it was still a hard country.

The coyote cried again. Gary shivered. The thought of entering that dark house, so full of memories, was not pleasant. A distant humming sound came across the quiet desert. Far across the black velvet shroud of the night came a flickering light, like a curious and probing finger. The light was moving with great speed along the graveled road that came from the main highway to the south. An erratic, popping, roaring noise came on the wind.

Gary grinned. It was probably Tucker C. "Tuck" Browne, riding his beloved Honda motorcycle full out, which was usually the only way he rode it. The darkness of the night seemed a little more friendly now. It was always that way when Tuck Browne came to see Gary. Tuck was a good, though temporary, distraction for the lure of the Lost Espectro.

Gary went into the house and turned on the kitchen and living room lights. Automatically he checked the supply of food in the refrigerator. He went out into the room off the back porch where the freezer was and took out additional supplies which he brought into the house. Tuck Browne had been on a marathon eating contest as far back as

Gary could remember and that had been a good part of his life, for the two boys had been friends since preschool days.

Gary went outside and called again for Lobo but there was no answering bark from the big dog. He looked up toward The Needle. Lobo was a prowler but he usually did not go too far into the canyons, no matter how inviting the hunting was. Lobo had always sensed that there was something wrong with those brooding canyons. He'd go along with Gary though, no matter how much he disliked doing so, his love for Gary overcoming his fear of the unknown.

Gary saw that the motorcyclist was charging along the fence line. Any minute he'd turn into the driveway past the windmill. Gary wisely took up a position where he could get into cover if Tuck made one of his spectacular stops anywhere near him. Tuck was gunning the motor in short, incessant bursts of power. The final act was about to begin.

2 The Mystery of The Needle

THE RUBBER SQUEALED as the tires of the Honda were forced into a hard, grinding turn from the road into the rutted driveway of the Cole Ranch. Tuck gunned the bike. The rear tire shrieked against the baked earth and gravel, and the Honda shot forward as though slung out of a catapult, boring through the dusk like an avenging angel. A bent figure could be seen, hanging onto the handlebars that were even with the driver's eye level. There was a grim determination in driver and bike as the two of them bounced across ruts and swung into the rather sharp turn just beyond the windmill. It was then that the tortured tires refused to grip the hard earth. The bike went into a spin, was wrenched out of it, then went into another sliding angle. Tuck gunned the roaring machine and it shot forward directly toward Gary. He sprinted for cover, vaulting over the low adobe wall just in front of the house.

Tuck Browne was magnificent. He shot past the wall, skidded in a wet patch near a faucet, then swung toward a sagging shed beyond the low barn. Gary watched in fascination as the bike bore down on the shed. Dust and smoke billowed up behind the Honda. "Hi, Gary!" screamed Tuck a fraction of a second before the Honda battered through the thin wall of the shed. "Brakes are gone!"

"Yeh," said Gary dryly. "They sure are."

Wood shattered and cracked, dust whirled up, the bike roared once more in futile protest, then was silent. Chickens squawked and skittered as they broke madly from the ruined shed and headed for the open desert, coyotes or no coyotes. In the sudden silence that followed the roaring onslaught of Tuck Browne on the hapless shed, the roof collapsed slowly and deliberately an instant after Tuck scrambled out of the wreckage.

Gary walked slowly toward the dramatic scene.

It was typical of Tuck Browne. The last time he arrived he had ripped through a line of Mrs. Cole's wash, taking the whole mess with him like a bridal train clean through a barbed wire fence into a filled earthen water tank.

Tuck unlimbered his thin six feet of frame and removed his helmet. He tentatively touched a split lip. "Cut three minutes off my last record out here," he said slowly.

"You figuring from town to the water tank or the shed, Tuck?"

Tuck rubbed a dusty jaw. "How much difference would that make?"

"Maybe ten seconds."

Tuck nodded solemnly. "Yeh. Well, anyway, I cut two minutes, fifty seconds off. You witness to that?"

"Keno."

Tuck eyed the shed. "Was your Dad thinking of tearing that down, Gary?"

"Not that I know of."

Tuck blinked his blue eyes. "Well, maybe I can talk him into it." He grinned. "Got the whole place to ourselves, eh, *amigo?*"

Gary glanced at the shed. "What's left of it."

Tuck walked slowly toward Gary. Tuck Browne never moved fast on foot if he could help it. He talked slowly, ate with deliberation, and never got to class or to work on time. He always seemed to be just short of standing still when he walked, that is, until he mounted the saddle of his Honda, at which time a strange metamorphosis took place, and the amiable, easygoing, lackadaisical being that was Tucker C. Browne became the personification of mad speed.

Tuck unzipped his jacket. "Got something new for you, Gary," he said. He glanced at the house. "You eat yet?"

"Yep."

Tuck's face fell. "Well, I figured on getting a bite."

"You eat at home?"

"Yes."

"Stopped at Bennie's Barbecue on the way?"

"Yes."

"Buy gas at Schick's Station?"

"A little," admitted Tuck.

"Had a Coke there and a bag of chips?"

Tuck nodded.

"And you *still* want to eat?"

Tuck looked positively mournful.

"Well, happens we have a pie left."

"What kind?" asked Tuck eagerly.

"Apple and raisin."

"You mean one apple and one raisin?"

"No, sonny, apple *and* raisin *together.*"

"Well, that's good enough."

"*Gracias,*" said Gary dryly.

"Wait'll I get my 'sickle' out of the shed," said Tuck. He slowly returned to the shed, and while Gary held up the shattered timbers, Tuck pulled the battered Honda from the wreckage. He eyed the bike carefully. "Not bad. Gotta get those brakes fixed one of these days. Could be dangerous."

"Yeh."

They walked together to the house. They went into the kitchen, and Gary placed half a pie before Tuck. He sat down and watched the pie vanish. "You said you had something new for me, Tuck."

Tuck nodded. His mouth was too full to talk. He jerked his head toward his jacket. "Inna pocket," he said.

Gary took out an odd-looking mass. It was a heavy lump of dirty wax, from which protruded four wicks at right angles to each other. Gary studied it, hefted it, turned it over and over, then looked quizzically at Tuck. Tuck swallowed. "Treasure-hunting candle," he said. "Got it from ol' Emilio Chavez. He said it was infallible."

"Go on."

Tuck cut another slice of pie. "Sure wish you had some whipped cream for this."

"Sorry. Go on!"

Tuck looked up. "On a dark, windy night you take that ball of wax to a place where you *think* treasure is. You light all four wicks, then with three *amigos,* each of you holding a wick, *below* the flame of course, you watch to see which wick burns longest in the wind. That long-burning wick points the general direction to the treasure."

"Yeh . . . *general* direction."

Tuck swallowed. "Well, anyway, by trial and error you finally get to where the treasure is."

"Man, you must have hit your head when you hit that shed."

"It should work, Gary!"

Gary shook his head. "I thought you might have found something that would be useful to us."

Tuck looked carefully about, as though someone might be eavesdropping. "There's something else about that candle."

"Shoot!"

Tuck's blue eyes were wide in his face. "It's partly made from dead man's fat, Gary," he whispered hoarsely.

"Oh, great!"

Tuck wet his lips. *"The fat from a man who was hung for murder!"*

A cold shiver crept up Gary's back, even though he was used to the mad ideas of Tuck Browne. He carefully placed the candle on the table and eyed it.

"Infallible," insisted Tuck.

Gary opened two Cokes. "I think I saw that light again, Tuck," he said quietly.

Tuck's jaws stopped moving. "You sure?"

Gary shrugged. "Pretty sure."

"Isn't it likely it could be any of the local ranchers up there hunting for strays maybe?"

Gary shook his head. "You know well enough no local man would shine a light up there, Tuck."

"Yeh." Tuck chewed reflectively. "Still, someone might have lighted a cigarette or something. You could see a match flare up quite a ways off. That's it! Someone lighted a cigarette up there!"

"But *who*, Tuck?"

Tuck's blue eyes studied Gary. "Who do you think it is?"

Gary walked to the window and looked out toward the huge, dark mass of The Needle. "That's the fourth time I've seen it this summer. No one lives up there. It isn't a fire. It comes and goes just like that! Always in just about the same place too."

"Yes?"

Gary turned. "Just about where that light shows is the best place around for anyone to keep an eye on a person coming up toward The Needle. From where they are situated they can see which way a person goes—into which canyon."

Tuck shoved back his plate. "Come on," he said quickly. "Tell me who you really think it is."

Gary leaned against the wall. "I'm not sure."

Tuck stood up and walked to the window. "Asesino," he said softly.

Again the cold chill came over Gary. *Asesino!* the half-real, half-mythical outlaw of the Espectros. Many of the local people did not believe he was still alive, or thought that he had long ago left the Espectros. There were others who were sure he had never left his hide-out. A man could live in those mountains and never be seen or found if he did not choose to be seen or found.

"How old would Asesino be now?" asked Tuck.

Gary half closed his eyes. "Let's see, he was about twenty years old when he committed his first murder. That was sometime in the twenties—about 1926 I think. Thirty-five years ago. He'd be about fifty-five years old if he were still alive."

"It's possible then," said Tuck quietly.

"No one has seen him for years. There have been rumors that he *has* been seen. I've never met anyone yet who said he had seen him in the last ten or fifteen years."

"Yeh," said Tuck thoughtfully. "But there have been murders up in there the past ten or fifteen years."

"Murders or accidents?"

"A man can't shoot himself in the back of the head with a rifle, can he?"

Tuck had Gary there. Two men, known to be looking for the Lost Espectro Mine, had vanished, and later one of them had been found lying in the middle of his camp with a bullet from a large-caliber rifle in the back of his skull. The coroner had verified the fact that the rifle had been fired from some distance, at an angle indicating that the marksman had been higher than the camp. The other man had never been found. Some people said he had killed his partner. Others said he had been killed by the same person who had killed his partner. No one really knew. That had been about twelve years ago.

Asesino had been a half-breed, or perhaps more than a half-breed. His father had been a white man, a deserter from the Army, who had married an Apache woman, whose father had been a Negro, or so the story went. Asesino then had been part white, part Indian, part Negro, and all bad. Asesino was not the man's real name. No one was sure what his real name had been. He had murdered his young wife in a drunken and jealous rage, then had fled toward the border. A posse had stopped him, and in the ensuing fight two possemen had died and Asesino had escaped. Trapped on three sides, he had retreated north, into the Espectros, which were an almost impenetrable fortress. He had committed several other killings, thus gaining the Spanish name he bore, a name that fitted him well—Asesino . . . The *Assassin.*

Asesino was one of the many legends about the Espectros, writing his legend in letters of blood. The man had the cunning and guile of a wolf, the cold ferocity of a grizzly, the stalking skill of a she-lion, the speed of an antelope, and the killing skill of a shark. The man had been an expert with rifle and pistol, bow and arrow, and knife—a man who could be set adrift in empty country without weapons and survive as his Apache ancestors had managed to survive in that wild and isolated country.

Tuck peered from the window. "Whoever it is might be watching for anyone traveling toward The Needle. He could see them easily enough during the day, no matter how they went in. Dust would rise from hooves or wheels. On moonlit nights it's almost as clear as daylight in there. On dark nights he could see can lights, or perhaps hear wheels and hooves. That place echoes like a tomb."

"Yeh . . . a tomb," said Gary. "You hit it, *amigo.*"

"Now, if two guys, say like you and me, were to sneak in there before moonrise, keeping quiet as the grave . . ."

"There you go again!"

"We might just spot something," continued Tuck calmly.

"Such as?"

"That loco sign you and your pa have been trying to spot all summer long."

Gary nodded. "As long as we don't go past The Needle."

"I wasn't aiming to!" said Tuck hastily.

It was an established fact that explorers, dudes, and ranchers had never been bothered *south* of The Needle. The canyons opened beyond the landmark, to the north, fanning out to penetrate deep into the Espectros. That was where the trouble always started. First the feeling that you were being watched. Then the warning shots. After that, you were on your own. . . .

"We can take the jeep," said Gary. "Drive without lights. Leave it on the playa south of the canyon where The Needle is. Walk in."

"How far?"

"Maybe a mile."

Tuck groaned. "Guess it can't be helped."

Gary put out the lights after he had managed to find a half dozen cartridges for his rifle. He loaded the weapon outside and stowed it in the back of the jeep. Tuck slid his six feet into the right front seat and sat with his bony knees up under his chin. It was very dark outside. Far across the quiet desert they could see sharp pinpoints of light. Headlights could be seen on the main highway into Cottonwood Wells. The glow from the lights of the town was visible above the rocky hills just south of it. But the Espectros were dark, a forbidding mass against the northern sky.

"Where's Lobo?" asked Gary's friend.

"*Quien sabe?* Who knows? I haven't seen him all day."

"He often take off like that?"

"Once in a while."

"Great! We sure could use him now."

Gary grinned. "You afraid, Tucker?"

Tuck nodded. "So are you, *amigo.*"

He was right. Gary started the jeep, drove out to the road, moving slowly because he had not turned on the headlights. He turned up a wide dry wash, and they bumped and clattered along it until they reached the playa, a place where sand, rock, and brush had been washed down the big canyon during flash floods. Gary stopped the engine and clambered out. Tuck got out and stretched. Gary took his rifle from the jeep, and the two of them stood there in the velvety darkness, listening to the dry soughing of the night wind through the mesquite.

Gary shrugged. He started forward, walking quietly, although no one near The Needle could possibly have heard footsteps on the playa. Still, it was said that Asesino had supernatural powers, or at least highly sensitive hearing and sight. As long as it was dark he could not see to shoot. But supposing he did not *stay* near The Needle?

The ground sloped upward toward the mouth of the canyon below The Needle. Higher and higher the two boys went until they could see the distant lights of The Wells clearly against the darkness of the desert.

There was a faint suggestion of moonlight in the east when Gary stopped. The huge bulk of The

Needle seemed to tower over them, although it was a good half-mile away. The wind whispered down the canyon, rustling the brush and murmuring against the canyon walls.

"Wait," said Tuck. "Maybe we ought to wait until tomorrow, Gary."

Gary turned. "You were the one who wanted to sneak in here before moonrise, keeping quiet as the grave."

"Did you have to say *that?*" hissed Tuck.

Gary walked on, peering ahead, past the dark bulk of The Needle. There wasn't much to see. He didn't really know why they had come in there, except that this weekend would probably be his last real chance to probe the mysteries of the place.

They squatted down behind a dike of rock that hid them completely except for their heads which protruded above the rock like the heads of two turtles encased in one shell.

Slowly the new moon came up, first flooding the wide desert in cold silvery light, then penetrating the canyon to light the western wall, although the eastern wall was still thick in shrouding shadows.

The two boys stared at that eastern wall. Somewhere on it was supposedly marked an ancient Spanish mining symbol. That same symbol was also supposed to be marked on the treasure chart left to Pete Cole by his father, but Pete had never been able to quite remember its exact location, or what it was. There were quite a few symbols in the old Spanish miner's code, some of them with varying meanings, some of them important, most of them of little importance. Although the existence of the symbol on the eastern canyon wall was doubtful, it was a well-known fact that there were many symbols scattered throughout the Espectros. Many men had seen them, and Gary's great-grandfather had made a chart of them and had tracked down their meanings. Gary had been given the chart by his father and he had memorized all of the cryptic markings. In fact it had been that very chart which had sparked his abiding interest in lost treasures and in the Lost Espectro Mine in particular.

Time dragged past, and then suddenly the moonlight began to creep along the eastern wall of the canyon, while two almost breathless boys stared at it until their eyes ached. Forgotten was the threat of Asesino and the unsolved mysteries of the Espectros.

The moonlight was now flooding the area where Gary had often thought he had seen something that was not a natural feature of the canyon.

Just as the moon completely illuminated the wall a mournful cry came drifting down the silent canyon on the cold night wind. It seemed to emanate from the very bowels of the upper canyon, or from an opened grave. Gary quickly levered a round of .30/30 into his rifle chamber, knowing full well that it would be of little use against the thing that had emitted that ghostly sound.

Tuck gripped his friend so hard by the arm that Gary winced. "Look!" he croaked.

The moonlight flooded the naked rock, and midway up the wall was a line, seemingly sharply etched—a long, long line that trended around a curved shoulder of rock. "Is it man-made or natural?" whispered Tuck.

Gary stared at it. "Only one way to find out," he said quietly.

"You're not going out there, are you?"

Gary did not answer. He leaned his rifle against the dike and walked around the end of the rock formation, keeping as much as possible in the shelter of scattered rocks and boulders and clumps of brush, until he could see that the line continued farther around the curve of rock. He wanted to see the end of it. Perhaps it was a gigantic arrow, pointing to the particular branch canyon where the Lost Espectro was. Perhaps it was a horizontal cross which indicated the same thing as the arrow, or a huge depiction of a bowie knife, also indicating a specific direction. *He had to know!*

The haunting cry came faintly down the canyon. Gary's throat went dry and his heart thudded against his ribs. He was getting awfully close to The Needle—too close perhaps. He could almost see where the line ended. He hurried forward, getting careless in his haste. He could hear Tuck panting along behind him.

The moon crept along the bald rock face. The moving light was a lodestone that Gary found impossible to resist. Forgotten were the warnings he had received.

He could see something now. He ran forward, head upraised, staring at that thin etched line on the whitish rock. Any second now he would know the secret.

The rifle shot crashed loudly in the stillness of the canyon. The slug whispered through the air just above Gary's head, and the harsh report of the rifle slammed back and forth between the canyon walls raising the hollow echoes.

Gary whirled and saw that he was beyond the

towering mass of The Needle. He took off down the canyon. His booted feet slammed against the hard ground like pistons and his breath came harshly in his dry throat. Fast as he was—and Gary had lettered in track at high school just the season before the summer—a gaunt figure passed him as though he were marking time. A strange, thin figure like an awkward crane, head outthrust, thin arms pumping up and down, big feet slapping the ground lightly, wheezing breath pumping from a gaping mouth, flew by him. Tuck Browne easily cleared a four-foot-high rock dike, the very picture of grace and motion, in ideal high-hurdle form, striking the ground like a feather on the far side, losing not a second of rhythm in his incredible burst of speed.

They passed the mouth of the canyon and headed toward the jeep. Gary reached it in time to see Tuck dive under it like a baseball player sliding home. He dragged the lean boy from beneath the jeep, shoved him into it, leaped in himself, turned on the ignition, shifted into first, and whirled the vehicle around, slamming it into second, ramming down on the accelerator to gather speed. He shifted into third as they reached the road and raced for home, raising a thick plume of dust behind them.

Not until they were inside the house with the thick door shut and barred did they look at each other with wide eyes. "It was Asesino all right," said Tuck.

"Did you see him?"

"Sure! Rose up like a jack-in-the-box atop The Needle! Aimed right at us! Lordy! Bullet nearly parted my hair, Gary!"

Cold sweat trickled down Gary's sides. He wiped the sweat from his face and grinned weakly. "Never saw you move so fast off that Honda."

Tuck nodded. "You and your letter," he scoffed. "Man, I was accelerating! Wasn't even out of second when I reached the jeep." Tuck walked to the refrigerator and opened it. He turned, and the light from inside the box accented his sharp features. "Come to think of it, Gary, I know how he got wise to us."

"Go on."

"The moonlight was shining off the windshield of the jeep like a sheet of silver. Could be seen for miles."

Gary leaned against the wall. "Never thought of that," he said.

Tuck selected a cold chicken leg. "Close," he said. He looked at Gary. "You don't suppose he'll come down here tonight, do you, Gary?"

Gary sat down on a chair and reached for a Coke from the refrigerator. "*Quien sabe?* Left my rifle up there."

"Great, oh great," murmured Tuck. "And Lobo isn't even here." He sank his fangs into the chicken leg.

Later, as they got into Gary's big bed, Tuck placed a hatchet under his pillow. "Might want to cut some wood later on," he said casually.

Gary nodded. He held up a butcher knife. "Or clean a rabbit," he said. His father's rifle was in town for repairs and the double-barreled shotgun had been loaned to a friend. Pete Cole usually carried his revolver in the pickup truck. It was going to be a long and lonely night.

The moonlight flooded through the window. The wind stirred the curtains.

"Kind'a cool in here, isn't it?" suggested Tuck.

Gary got up and walked to the window. He looked up toward The Needle. It was bright with moonlight. He slid down the window and, as he turned toward the bed, his eye caught a quick spark of light, high on the canyon wall beyond the huge mass of The Needle. He turned quickly. But there was no sign of light now. Nothing but the silvery wash of the cold moonlight on the silent canyon and the brooding Needle.

3 Stranger in the Dawn

THE INCESSANT BARKING of a dog aroused Gary from a deep sleep. He sat up suddenly, startled and confused. He recognized Lobo's deep voice. Gary thrust his legs from beneath the blanket and stood up. It was still dark outside and he had no idea what time it was. He padded to the door of the bedroom and opened it to step into the hallway. Lobo was still barking furiously.

He walked across the dark living room and peered through a window. It was dark all right but there was a faint suggestion of dawn in the sky. He could locate Lobo by the sound of his barking but he could not see the big dog.

"What is it?" asked Tuck from the hallway.

"I don't know," answered Gary. He peered from one side of the front yard to the other, seeing nothing that would alarm the big dog, but he knew well enough that Lobo wasn't a habitual barker.

Gary eased the bar from the door and slowly opened it. He stepped outside and flattened himself against the front wall of the house. He could hear Tuck's quick and irregular breathing just behind him. "I got the hatchet," said Tuck.

"Shut up!" hissed Gary.

Objects in the yard were dimly outlined against the graying sky. The windmill was still. Gary crouched and walked along the porch until he was at the northern end of it. He unconsciously glanced toward the Espectros, seeing nothing but their huge and indistinct outline against the sky. A cold whisper of the dawn wind crept along the desert, rustling the leaves of the trees beside the house. The vanes of the windmill hummed a little.

Lobo suddenly stopped barking. A low growl came from him. He was near the low stock shed north of the house. Gary could just make him out. There was a pick handle leaning against the side of the house. Gary gripped it and started toward the dog. As long as Lobo was alert no one would bother Gary.

He was within twenty feet of Lobo when the dog suddenly stopped growling. Gary had an uneasy feeling of being watched. He turned quickly, not really expecting to see anything out of the usual, but when he did, his heart seemed to skip a beat and his throat suddenly went dry.

A hatless man stood beyond the fieldstone wall looking directly at him. He had a rifle in his hands. Gary froze. Every instinct within him cried out to run, run, run! He glanced at Lobo. The big dog was still alert, watching the stranger, but he wasn't growling as he should have been.

Gary looked again at the silent, menacing figure, hoping that it was a mirage conjured up by his vivid imagination. It was still there. It moved. "Stay where you are!" said Gary. He raised the pick handle as though it were a rifle.

The figure raised the rifle it held. Gary's throat seemed to close up and his stomach turned to water. "Take it easy, Gary," said the man. "Found your rifle up the canyon late last night."

Gary stared at him. "Who is it?" he asked.

"Lije Purtis, Gary. You know me."

Gary nodded. Lije was a local character. A man

who prowled the local countryside at all hours of the day and night, sleeping wherever he happened to be, living off handouts, or working just enough to pay for the next few meals. Lije never bothered anyone. That was why Lobo had stopped barking as soon as he had recognized the man.

"You want the rifle, Gary?" asked Lije.

"Sure, Lije." There was no use in talking sharply to the man for coming there in the predawn darkness with a rifle in his hands. It would do no good. "You hungry, Lije?" he asked.

"Always am, Gary."

"Come on in then." Gary patted Lobo. "Where have *you* been, you bum?" he asked.

Lobo barked shortly. He was a powerfully muscled dog, like a mastiff, with a brown and white pelt and a black face, a combination of several breeds.

Lije climbed over the fence and shambled toward them. "I see him now and then in the canyons," he said.

That was another odd thing about Lije. Lije would go into the Espectros, without water, food, blankets, or arms, stay as long as he liked, then wander out again, perhaps on the remote north side, or the wild east and west sides, sometimes on the more accessible south side. The local Apaches knew him well and took care of him when he wandered their way. "Mind-Gone-Far" they called him, for he was protected by the gods.

Lije handed Gary the rifle. He smiled vacantly, revealing his crooked yellow teeth and the gaps between them. His washed-out eyes never left Gary's face. Gary always had an odd feeling that Lije was enjoying some vast and secret joke of his own when he looked at people. Tuck always said that he wasn't quite sure who was crazy, Lije Purtis, or the rest of the world.

"Is it your rifle, Gary?" called Tuck.

"Yes."

"How did you know it was Gary's rifle?" asked Tuck of Lije.

"It is, ain't it?" said Lije.

"I know," said Tuck patiently. "But how did *you* know?"

No one seemed to know whether Lije could read and write. No one knew just how much Lije did know.

"It's Gary's," said Lije simply.

Gary looked at Tuck. Tuck shrugged. "Where did you find it, Lije?" asked Tuck. His shrewd blue eyes studied the man.

"Up the canyon."

"Where?"

"Behind a rock ledge. Lying on the ground it was."

An odd feeling came over Gary. He worked the lever. A spent cartridge case tinkled on the hard ground. Five more fresh cartridges were ejected from the rifle before it was emptied. He had loaded it the evening before with six rounds. "Did you shoot it, Lije?" he asked quietly.

Lije's eyes widened. "I don't even know *how* to shoot one, Gary," he said. "You know that!"

Gary nodded. He looked up toward The Needle now being bathed in the cold gray light. There was no use asking Lije how he happened to be up there during the night, or how he had stumbled upon the rifle—if he *had* just *stumbled* upon it.

"What's wrong, Gary?" asked Tuck.

Gary turned. "One round was fired. Lije didn't fire it. You follow me?"

Tuck rubbed his lean jaw. "Yeh," he said shamefacedly. "Maybe it fell over and discharged. Maybe that was the shot that stampeded us. I had an idea all the time it was that."

"Oh sure," said Gary dryly. "Seems to me you said something like this when I asked you if you had seen Asesino: 'Sure! Rose up like a jack-in-the-box atop The Needle! Aimed right at us! Lordy! Bullet nearly parted my hair, Gary!' "

Tuck flushed. "Well, a guy gets nervous like."

"Sure does." Gary looked at Lije. "You see anyone else up there, Lije?"

"No."

"You sure?"

The veil over the faded eyes was more pronounced. "You asked me if I was hungry, Gary," he said petulantly.

Gary nodded. "Sure, Lije." There was no use in going further with the man. Gary slowly reloaded the rifle. Lije shambled toward the house and walked in as though it were his own.

Tuck studied Gary. "Well?"

Gary shrugged. "It could have been my rifle that went off by accident. I had loaded the chamber and then leaned it against the rock dike. Careless of me."

"That's not like you, Gary," admitted Tuck. "Now me, *I'd* do a thing like that."

"Lije isn't supposed to know how to shoot a rifle," said Gary thoughtfully. "But supposing he did?"

"You mean he might have shot at us?"

"I mean, maybe he shot it sometime later during

the night. Maybe someone really *did* shoot at us in there. But how can we know that?"

Tuck nodded. "I've always said Lije probably knows a lot more than we give him credit for. He's smart enough not to have to work and yet he gets by. The rest of us have to work hard for a living."

"Well, we'll never know," said Gary. He looked again at The Needle. More mystery. The place seemed to breed mysteries as it did thunderstorms in the summer and pouring flash floods in the fall and winter. "I'd like to know what Lije sees in there."

"Or *what* sees Lije," added Tuck softly.

Gary shivered. "Let's eat. We've got a long, hard day ahead of us."

Gary was kept busy cooking for the two guests. Voracious as Tucker C. Browne was, he was an amateur compared to the thin and gaunt Lije. Tuck finally conceded defeat after Lije started on his third plateful of flapjacks. When they had finished eating, Lije arose. He looked at Gary. "Map," he said.

Gary knew what Lije wanted. He went into his room and brought out the large local map he had bought the summer before and upon which he had made notes, corrections, and additions for his personal quest for the Lost Espectro. Lije knew Gary was interested in the Lost Espectro. Gary placed the map on the cleared table, and Lije leaned over it. He nodded in satisfaction. Lije might not be able to read but he knew well enough the shape and size of the Espectros. He placed a dirty broken fingernail on a watercourse and traced it to a huge bluff that had forced the watercourse to change its channel. "Arrastres," he said. He stabbed his finger down hard, denting the thick paper.

Gary stared at the map. The watercourse flowed out into the wild desert southeast of the range. He had been in that area the year before as wrangler for a small party of dudes who had been looking for cliff dwellings. They had found a few crumbling structures, but Gary had not seen any arrastres in there. Arrastres were primitive ore-crushing mills, used by the early Spanish miners to crush the gold ore. Where there were arrastres, there should be, or had been, gold or silver mines. He looked up at Lije. Gold and silver meant nothing to this child of nature. There was no expression on the man's thin face, but Gary realized that Lije was paying for his meal in the only way he knew.

Lije walked to the door. He turned and eyed the two boys. "Be careful," he said. He swiftly drew his left hand across his throat in a gruesome gesture. "*Asesino!*" Then he was gone from the house.

Tuck shuddered a little. "Cheerful *hombre*," he said.

Gary eyed the map again. "Arrastres," he said thoughtfully.

"Maybe he was kidding us."

"No."

"Then we may have found a clue to the mines!"

"Arrastres weren't always near the mines, Tuck. The arrastres used in crushing the ore of the old Peralta Mines, believed to be the lode that the Dutchman found in the Superstitions, were quite a distance from the mines. The ore was brought down in *aparejos* by mule train."

"Well, it's better than nothing!"

Gary grinned. "You can say that again. You want to take a crack at it today?"

"That's why I came out here, *amigo*. After last night I want no part of The Needle for some time."

"Yeh," said Gary dryly.

They were loading the jeep when the wind shifted. Gary quickly raised his head. "Listen!" he said.

The sound of a car engine came to them from the northwest. Gary whirled. There was only one road in there—the road he and Tuck had traveled the night before. It went in toward the western ramparts of the Espectros, then ended at Massacre Springs.

"Dust," said Tuck.

A thin wraith of dust hung over the desert, moving toward the northwest.

"Wonder who it is," said Gary.

"Which way did Lije go?"

"*Quien sabe?* He can't drive anyway."

"Sure, sure! Lije can't shoot! Lije can't read! Lije can't write! Lije can't drive!"

Gary turned. "What do you mean?"

"I've always said Lije knows a lot more than folks give him credit for, Gary. How do we know he isn't in that car right now?"

"He can't drive, I tell you!"

Tuck lowered his voice. "Sure, *he* can't drive, but he can sure ride with someone else who *can* drive."

Gary was puzzled. "I see what you mean."

"So we go chasing off after a wild goose to the *east* of the Espectros for some beat up old arrastres while Ol' Lije goes the other way."

Gary whirled again. He snatched his father's binoculars from the jeep and ran to the windmill. He swiftly climbed the ladder to the platform at the top, took the glasses from their case, and raised them to his eyes, focusing them on the dust that seemed to be moving more swiftly. But the vehicle was below a low rise of ground, and there was no place where the road crossed an open area where Gary might catch a fleeting glimpse of it. He slowly descended the ladder. "No fish," he said to Tuck.

"Mysteriouser and mysteriouser," said the lean one.

The telephone jangled insistently. Gary ran to the house and picked up the phone. "Gary?" his father said. "Listen! Sue Browne wants to come out and spend the day with you and Tuck."

"Oh, Lord," groaned Gary.

"Your mother will drop her off up at the highway in about half an hour. Pick her up there. I wasn't sure you'd be home yet. Glad I caught you."

"Yep," said Gary.

"She's a nice kid," said Pete Cole. "She'll be good company for you boys."

"Oh sure, Dad."

"O.K. Pick her up in about half an hour to forty-five minutes. 'Bye, son."

Gary replaced the phone on its cradle. Tuck thrust his owlish face into the room. "Who was it? Asesino? Hawww!" he brayed.

"Worse," said Gary. "That was my father. Seems like your beloved cousin, Miss Susan Browne, is to spend the day with us."

Tuck paled. "We still got time to pull out?"

"My mother will drop her off up at the highway. We have to pick her up there."

Tuck seemed trapped. "Let's vamoose!" he said.

"My father told me to pick her up. I'll have to do it, Tuck."

"Why'd you have to answer that phone anyway?"

"How did I know Sue was back in town?"

"Yeh. She was away at some summer camp or something. Sure was quiet around town with her gone. By golly, I'll just bet she knew what we were going to do! I wouldn't put it past her, *amigo!*"

Gary nodded. "And just the day we get a solid lead on the Lost Espectro too."

They walked outside to the jeep. Gary whistled for Lobo. The huge dog leaped into the back seat and settled himself with a proprietary air. Gary drove out onto the gravel road and toward the main highway. Gloom rode along with them. "Sue Browne," groaned Tuck. "Sometimes I'm not even sure she's kin to me. No one else in the whole family is quite like Sue, odd as they all are."

"I'll buy that," said Gary gloomily.

They waited at the junction of the highway and the gravel road. In a short time they saw the familiar, battered green pickup truck. Mrs. Cole drew off on the shoulder of the road. The look in her blue eyes was sufficient for her to warn Gary without opening her mouth. Mrs. Cole well knew the effect Sue Browne had on the boys.

The fifteen-year-old object of all the trouble got out of the truck, waved good-bye to Mrs. Cole and walked quickly toward the jeep. She opened her mouth in a wide smile, and the early morning sun glinted on the braces she wore. "Brought my own lunch, Gary!" she cried happily. "Got some extra for the Hungry Dragon too!"

"That's *me,*" said Tuck unhappily. "I'd rather go hungry, so help me, Gary."

Sue was getting taller, Gary noted. But she was still shaped something like Tuck, all odds and ends and angles. She had dark brown hair, cut short and a battered sombrero was perched on the back of her head.

"Gary!" called Mrs. Cole.

He got out of the jeep. "Get into the back with Lobo," he said casually to Sue.

Sue had one beautiful feature—a pair of big brown eyes that seemed to dominate her face. If a fellow didn't look at her braces, tip-tilted nose, and freckles too closely, she'd almost be considered pretty because of her eyes.

Mrs. Cole leaned toward Gary. "It wasn't my idea, Gary," she said in a low voice. "But now that she is here, I want you boys to treat her nicely."

"Yes, ma'am."

She studied him. "What happened last night?"

"Nothing."

She eyed him closely. She had an uncanny knack of knowing when things went wrong with Gary. "Are you sure?"

"Yes, ma'am."

"Where are you going today?"

"Over to the southeast side of the Espectros."

She smiled in relief. "Thank heaven for that! I thought you might be foolish enough to go poking about in the canyon near The Needle."

"Not today, Mother."

She half closed her eyes. "I see. What's up at the east end?" she asked quickly.

"I thought we might find some Indian relics."

"Nothing on the Lost Espectro though?"

"Well," admitted Gary, "if we find anything we sure won't just walk away from it."

"Your father and I will be home late this evening. Can you take Sue home?"

"Tuck can take her on his Honda."

"No! Absolutely not! *You* bring her home."

"All right, Mother."

The pickup turned and moved back toward The Wells. Gary shrugged, cleared his throat, then plodded toward the jeep. Sue was tucked in beside the bulk of the dog. She was all smiles. "Sure will be fun," she said.

"Yeh," said Tuck. He sagged lower in his seat.

Gary did not talk as he drove off to the east. Sue Browne had a hide like a rhinoceros when it came to figuring she was not wanted.

"Where to?" she asked brightly.

"East," said Gary shortly.

"I know. But where?"

"Got a lead on some Indian relics near a dry stream."

"Nothing on the Lost Espectro?"

Gary looked out of the corner of his eye at Tuck. Sue was a talker, sure enough. Tuck yawned. "Hey," he said suddenly. "You wearin' perfume, Susie?"

She seemed to swell up a little, Gary noted in the rear-vision mirror. "A little, Tuck," she coyly admitted. "Why?"

Tuck yawned again. "For a minute I thought it

was Lobo," he said. He closed his eyes as though to sleep.

She had walked right into it. Sue flushed and looked quickly away. She'd be quiet now until they reached the watercourse at least. Still, Gary couldn't help but feel a little sorry for her. She wasn't a bad kid if she'd only learn to keep her mouth shut.

4 Canyon of the Skull

THE SUN WAS IN FULL SPATE against the eastern side of the Espectros. Gary had stopped the jeep against a perpendicular wall of rock. As he turned the engine off, the silence, with the exception of the softly murmuring wind, seemed to descend upon the empty countryside. The wide gap of the watercourse was to the north of them. Lobo, already on his way, was threading easily through the cactus and greasewood clumps.

"You sure that's the place, Gary?"

Gary nodded. He tapped the side of his head. "The map is in here."

"Lots of room for it in there," cracked Sue. She swallowed hard as she saw the looks they shot at her.

"Funny, oh *funny*," said Tuck.

"Just what are we looking for?" she asked.

There was no use in trying to deceive Sue Browne. She had the native shrewdness of the Brownes. "Arrastres," said Gary.

She nodded wisely. "Makes sense. I never could see fooling around The Needle. That so-called mining symbol in there isn't even a mining symbol from what I've heard. Now . . ." Her voice died away as she saw the intent looks on the faces of her companions.

"Just what do you mean, Sue?" asked Tuck.

"Well, when I was at summer camp, the *cocinero* there was an old man who said he had often looked in the Espectros for the lost mines. He said it was a waste of time looking about The Needle. He said he had heard about that sign in there you were supposed to see about four o'clock in the afternoon in August or September. Well, according to him it was just a big split in the rock."

"He knows so much," said Tuck angrily.

She placed her hands on her slim hips. "Sure he does! He said it wasn't likely those old miners would make a signboard pointing *right* to the canyon the mine was *in*. That would be a little more than stupid, wouldn't it?"

Tuck looked at Gary; Gary looked right back at Tuck.

Sue slung a canteen strap over her shoulder and picked up her big lunch bag, fastening it to her belt. "So, where there are arrastres, there must be a mine. Right?"

"Right!" they chorused.

"Then what are we waiting for?" Sue took off briskly.

Tuck folded an arm across his lean stomach, rested his other elbow on it, then cupped his chin in his hand. He watched his cousin trudging through the cactus and greasewood. "Well, I'll be drowned in sheep dip," he said slowly.

Gary took the rifle, binoculars, and haversack from the jeep. "Get the rest of the stuff," he said. "Let's give her a good lead. Maybe she'll get lost."

"With *that* lunch! Sue isn't much for looks or anything else, but her mother can put up the best lunch you ever saw, *amigo!*"

They followed the slim girl through the growths. Lobo was waiting for them at the mouth of the dry watercourse. He trotted ahead of them as they fought their way through a tangle of catclaw. By the time they reached more open ground the heat of the day was pouring into the narrow canyon ahead of them.

"How far ahead?" asked Tuck.

Gary pointed to the huge, naked bluff that seemed to block the passage of the stream about one mile ahead of them.

"Funny I never heard of arrastres being in here," said Tuck. "Seems like someone would have spoken about them."

It didn't take them long to find out why the arrastres had been a secret for so long. Detritus had fallen from the huge overhanging walls of the canyon and had formed treacherous slopes of loose sliding rock, interlaced with catclaw and wait-a-bit bush that tore at their clothing and ripped their skin. Only Lobo seemed immune to the sharp thorns. At one point it seemed as though they would have to turn back until Lobo casually trotted around behind a huge split boulder. When they followed him they found themselves in a sort of natural passageway, affording barely enough room to squeeze through. After a zigzag passage they came out upon a flat rock area where they could see the bluff towering above them. Here the passage of the stream bed seemed unimpeded.

"Must have been easier to get in here years

ago," said Gary thoughtfully. "No wonder these arrastres have never been seen in modern times."

"Except by Lije," said Tuck.

Sue turned. "Lije Purtis?" she asked.

Tuck nodded. "We talked to him this morning. He brought Gary's rifle back."

"From where?" she asked. "I never saw Gary leave that precious .30/30 of his anywhere."

Gary could have hit Tuck with a rock. That girl had an inquiring nose like an anteater.

"From where?" asked Sue again. She eyed them. "I'll bet you went into the canyon near The Needle yesterday sometime."

"You know a lot," scoffed Tuck.

"What happened in there? How come Gary left his rifle in there?"

"Nothing happened in there!" snapped Tuck.

"Then you *were* in there!" she said triumphantly.

She had trapped Tuck neatly, and that wasn't easy to do. She sat down on a rock and studied them.

"So help me," said Tuck. "If you didn't have that lunch I'd leave you here."

"You *can't* leave me here! Besides, I'm not afraid of Asesino."

"Oh no?" snarled Tuck. "If he took a shot at you like he did at us last night you'd run like a striped bird, you would. . . ." His voice died away. A panicky look came over his thin face. "Oh, Lord," he continued. "Now I did it."

Her eyes sparkled. "I wish I had been there!"

"So help me, Sue," breathed Tuck, "if you open your mouth around my folks—or Gary's folks—about this, I'll never talk to you again!"

She half closed her eyes. "Well, I'll consider it," she said.

Gary picked up his rifle and walked on. He would willingly have left both of them behind. He followed Lobo through the brush and to the bank of the dry watercourse. Up and down he went, then across to the far bank and up and down that. Nothing, absolutely nothing. The words of Tuck came back to him: "So we go chasing off after a wild goose to the *east* of the Espectros for some beat up old arrastres while Ol' Lije goes the other way."

The others joined him, and for two hours they searched every foot of the ground with no results. The sun was at its zenith when they stopped. "Hopeless," said Tuck. "I was right all the time."

They ate their lunch in gloomy silence. Sue didn't eat much; she never did. She left the spoils to Tuck, whose appetite was never spoiled by anything. It was almost a relief for the two boys to see her fade off into the brush. Gary sent Lobo after her.

"Blind alley again," said Tuck around a mouthful of cake.

"Yeh." Gary shook his head. "Maybe Sue is a hoodoo."

"Figures."

A wild shriek echoed through the quiet canyon. Gary moved like a flash, snatching up his rifle, then hurdling a rock. He dashed through the clinging brush heedless of the piercing thorns. He twisted his ankle on a loose rock footing, then burst into a clearing high on the slope. He could see a dim figure beyond the clearing, jumping up and down. It was Sue. Gary levered a round into the Winchester, then suddenly lowered it. Lobo had come out of the brush and was trotting toward Gary with what passed for a pleased look on his ugly black face. Nothing serious could be wrong with Sue. Gary walked toward her. She was dancing about like an awkward marionette on a string. "Eureka!" she shrieked. Her voice echoed through the canyon like that of a banshee.

Gary winced at the piercing sound of her voice. She was pointing down at her feet. Gary leaned his rifle against a tree after emptying the chamber. He eyed a shallow circular trough worn into the hard ground. To one side was a narrow trough that angled off toward the dry bed of the watercourse. The circular trough was rimmed with low piles of material. There was little doubt in Gary's mind as to what he was looking at.

"Is it what we're looking for?" asked Sue.

He looked up at her and smiled. "It's an arrastre all right. The circular trough was made by burros pulling a stone to crush the ore. The other trough brought in water."

Tuck came toward them. "What is it?" he called out.

"See for yourself, Tuckie!" cried Sue.

"Tuckie!" said Tuck. He rolled his eyes upward. He looked down at the arrastre. "What is it, Gary?"

"Arrastre, Tuck."

"You sure?"

Gary nodded. He looked up at the towering walls of the isolated canyon. "What else could it be?"

"Yeh," said Tuck. He looked at Sue. "Stumbled on it, eh, Susie?"

She shook her head. "Look," she said. She led the way to a rock at one side of a scarcely definable trail. There was a faint dark mark upon it. "This mark was evidently made by a mule shoe striking it. I found the trail, then found several other marks like the first one and walked right to here."

"Just like that?"

She nodded. "Just like that." She felt in a pocket of her Levi's and brought out a curved and badly rusted piece of metal. She held it up. "Found this halfway up the trail."

Gary took it from her hand. "Piece of a burro shoe," he said quietly. "Too small for a mule or a horse."

"Now what?" asked Tuck.

It was very quiet in the canyon except for the humming of the wild bees and the soft soughing of the wind that rustled the leaves. Gary walked to the west, parting the brush. Fifty feet from the first arrastre he stumbled into a hollow in the ground. It was another arrastre. There wasn't much doubt about their age. No modern miners would have made them. But Gary had seen other arrastres in other parts of the Espectros and they had led to nothing. But this was a part of the Espectros hardly visited by anyone. Gary had never heard any talk about mines in this area.

Sue and Tuck came up behind him. "Scatter," he said. "See what else we can find. Don't get too far from each other. Lobo, go with Sue."

An hour passed slowly, then Tuck came to Gary,

holding another badly rusted burro shoe in his hand. The ends of the shoe had been flared out. He handed it to Gary. "Found it up the trail. Pretty rough in there. I poked around but it's impossible to see where the trail goes. What do you think of this shoe?"

"It's definitely of Spanish pattern. See the flared ends? They still make the same pattern shoe in Mexico to this day though."

"Big help, eh?" said Tuck disgustedly. "Could have been left here at most any time."

Sue came through the brush. "I don't think so, Tuck. If they don't make that type of shoe around here, it isn't likely anyone would bring up a burro or mule from Mexico to go joyriding around here in the past thirty or forty years, is it?"

"There she goes again," said Tuck.

Gary hefted the shoe. "She's got something there. With this and the arrastres we don't need much more proof that miners were in here. Spanish miners . . ."

"But no trail," said Tuck.

Gary nodded. He looked up at the forbidding south wall of the deep canyon. "There has to be a trail!" He walked to the south, following the faint trace of the ancient trail. When he reached the place where it petered out he could see that

Tuck had been right. It just vanished completely. He got down on his hands and knees and peered through the brush trying to find a continuation of the trail. He tried the old trick of half closing his eyes and then suddenly opening them, hoping to catch an elusive glimpse of the trail, but the trail was just as elusive as the mysterious light he had seen several times up the canyon beyond The Needle. There was no trail, and yet there *had* to be one. If there were arrastres there must be a mine, or mines, even if they had been worked out.

It was a downhearted boy who walked back to the others. "I can't figure it out," he said.

Tuck had the field glasses, and with them he was slowly scanning the canyon wall inch by inch. "I thought perhaps we'd see a trace of another canyon opening into this one," he said, "but this country is so rough and broken up it's impossible to say whether there are any other canyons beyond this one."

"There's something else over here!" called out Sue.

They walked over to see her standing in front of what looked like tumbled walls of stonework. The walls had been formed in a small rectangle, hardly more than ten or twelve feet long by six or seven feet wide. Amidst the litter in the middle of it protruded several broken poles. "Rafters," said Gary. "The roof collapsed inside the building, whatever it was."

"There's one way to find out what it was," said Sue. She placed a long leg over the wall and began to pitch out stones and beams, heedless of the two boys. They started to help her. They uncovered several rusted pots, a broken bucket, a skillet thoroughly eaten through by rust, a pair of husk sandals and a broken pick handle. Gary sat back on his heels and shoved back his hat. "Doesn't mean much," he said. "You can't really tell how long this stuff has been in here. Might have been in the last twenty years. Nothing to show Spanish origin."

"And nothing to sell to a museum," said Tuck. He shook his head.

"Look," said Sue in a hollow voice. She pointed just beyond the back wall. Something white showed in the brush. There wasn't any doubt as to what it was. Gary stepped over the crumbling wall and knelt beside the skeleton. The clothing was rotten with exposure, and there was nothing to indicate how long it had been there. One part was missing—the skull.

Sue was a little pale. "It's getting late," she said. "Maybe we'd better head back."

Tuck grinned. "Heck, it's not more than two o'clock, Susie. Gary and I were thinking of staying until after dark."

Gary looked up toward the canyon wall. Through the moving leaves of the scrub trees and the brush he could see a huge boulder with a whitish excresence atop it. Something drew him toward that boulder, and he walked about fifty yards before he stood in front of it looking up at the whitish object. It was a bleached skull. He climbed up beside it and picked it up. A cold feeling of fear shot through him. The back of the skull had evidently been shattered by something. A bullet from a heavy-caliber rifle . . .

The hollow eyeholes of the gruesome relic stared up at him as though in warning. Gary suddenly had an uneasy feeling that he was being watched. He looked quickly about. There was no sign of life. He wet his dry lips and slid down to the ground, still holding the skull. He walked through the shadowy grove of trees to the tumbled ruins. Sue's breath caught in her throat as she saw what Gary held in his hands.

Tuck was squatting by the headless skeleton. "Hey," he said over his shoulder. "I found a belt buckle. Initials J. B." He turned to look at them and his face blanched. "Where'd you get that?" he said hollowly.

"Up there on that boulder," said Gary.

It seemed unnaturally quiet just at that moment. An uneasy sort of a stillness had closed in on them.

Something rustled. The two boys darted glances at Sue. "I found a newspaper," she said in a very small voice. "A Tucson paper dated July 10, 1949."

"About twelve years ago," said Tuck. He looked at Gary and Gary knew well enough what he was thinking. Twelve years ago two men had been looking for The Lost Espectro. They had vanished and one of them had been found some weeks later with what appeared to be a bullet hole from a large-caliber rifle through the back of his skull. *The other man had never been found.* Gary looked down at the skull in his hands. *Maybe he had been found at last.*

"Come to think of it," said Tuck. "It *is* getting late."

Sue nodded vigorously.

Gary hefted the skull. No animal had hauled that skull from the body to place it high on that boulder facing toward the camp. It just wasn't natural. Maybe it had been placed as a warning. Whoever guarded the hidden secrets of the

Espectros couldn't be everywhere at once to do his self-appointed duty. Maybe he left these little relics around to hold the fort while he was busy elsewhere.

A thick, dark cloud came between the sun and the mountains, and darkness seemed to fill the canyon like the settling veil of night. Without a word the three explorers turned to walk back toward the arrastres. Gary picked up his rifle. None of them spoke. The wind increased, moaning eerily through the canyon.

Lobo led the way, trotting easily, but even the big mastiff seemed a little nervous. It wasn't until they were threading the narrow, natural passageway that the dog stopped suddenly and looked back beyond the three of them. His hackles rose and he bared his strong, yellow teeth. A low, fierce growling came deep from his throat.

Tuck grabbed Sue by the arm and shoved her ahead. "Get out of the way," he said fiercely. He turned to stand beside Gary. Gary loaded his rifle. They could hear Sue's stumbling footsteps. Lobo growled again. "Go on, Tuck," said Gary quietly. "You'd better stick with Sue."

"What about you?"

"I've got the rifle and Lobo."

Tuck swallowed hard. "I'll stay," he said hoarsely.

"Go with Sue!" snapped Gary.

Tuck moved on. Lobo moved quietly back along the passageway, ears flat and head thrust forward. Gary wet his lips. It was almost like dusk in the canyon. He glanced up at the cloud. It was then that he saw a movement high above him. "Lobo!" he yelled. The dog darted back. Gary ran like a deer. A moment later a huge rock crashed in the narrow passageway, scattering shards far and wide. One of them struck Gary in the middle of the back. The sound of the crashing rock echoed through the canyon.

Gary tore through the clinging brush, heedless of the clutching thorns. He saw Tuck and Sue far ahead of him and an intense loneliness gripped him. He slipped and fell on the loose detritus, almost landing in a deep gully to one side. He scuttled back up the slope and plunged toward the open area to the east. He reached a flat area and turned to see Lobo standing on the detritus looking back into the inner canyon. He was growling again. "Come on, Lobo!" he cried. The big dog turned and trotted toward his master.

Gary looked up at the place the rock had fallen from. There was no sign of life up there; nothing to indicate that the rock had been pushed by human hands. An icy finger seemed to trace the length of his spine. If Gary had not seen the first movement of the falling rock he would certainly have been crushed by it.

He walked slowly down out of the wide mouth of the canyon. Far ahead of him were the figures of Tuck and Sue. It seemed as though every time he found a clue to the mystery of the Lost Espectro Mine, something interfered. Maybe it was true that there was a curse on the Lost Mine of the Espectros. The local Mexicans called it *Oro Encantado,* or Haunted Gold. Gary was beginning to believe they had just cause for their belief.

The first drops of rain struck them as they climbed into the jeep. In a few minutes the rain was sheeting down, and by the time Gary reached the main highway he had been forced to use low gear and four-wheel drive. The battered jeep groaned and lurched through the thickening adobe mud. Behind them the Espectros were sheathed in mist and rain, and thunder pealed and rolled through the hidden gorges.

Sue shivered. "I'm glad we got out of there when we did," she said.

Tuck peeled off his jacket and handed it to her. "Yeh," he said quietly. He looked at Gary. "What do you think Lobo was growling at?"

"*Quien sabe?*"

"I had a feeling all the time we were in there that we were being watched," said Tuck.

Gary nodded. He glanced toward the mountains. "There's something in there all right."

"Like what?" asked Sue.

"Gold," said Gary.

"And ghosts."

Something rattled in the bottom of the jeep. Sue gingerly picked up the bullet-shattered skull. "'Alas, poor Yorick,'" she said. "'I knew him well.'"

"There she goes again," said Tuck. "I knew it!"

It was dark by the time they reached the Cole Ranch. Rain slanted down steadily and a cold wind drove across the soaked desert. The three of them took the relics into the little room next to Gary's bedroom. "I'll tell my father about what we found," said Gary. "He'll probably notify the sheriff about the skull."

"What do you think the sheriff will do?" asked Tuck.

Gary shrugged. "They never solved the death of the other man who was found with a hole through the back of his head. It isn't likely they'll find out any more about this one."

Tuck took his jacket from Sue. "Well, I've got to get back. You taking Sue home, Gary?"

"Yes."

Sue's braces glistened in the light as she smiled widely. Lots of girls in The Wells would have liked to ride in Gary Cole's jeep on a wet night even if the top did leak.

"It was my mother's idea," said Gary hastily.

"Yeh . . . that's what I figured," said Tuck.

Gary gave Sue a jacket and one of his mother's raincoats. As they walked out to the jeep they heard the roaring of the Honda, and Tuck Browne slithered along the road heading toward the highway, riding as though the Devil were treading on his coattails.

Halfway to the main highway, Sue kept looking back over her shoulder with a puzzled look on her face. "Is there an air-warning beacon on or near The Needle, Gary?" she asked.

He shook his head, intent on his driving.

"Are you sure?"

"Positive! Why do you ask?"

She eyed him. "Because I just saw a flickering light up the canyon past The Needle."

He nearly went off the road, turned the wheel into the direction of the skid and brought the jeep back to the center of the road. He braked it to a halt and turned to look back. The Needle thrust itself up, looming in the wet darkness. There was no sign of a light up that mysterious canyon.

"What's wrong, Gary?" she asked.

He shook his head. "Nothing." He started the jeep and drove on. The lure of the Espectros was opposed to the mystery and death that shrouded them. It had held his great-grandfather's interest and his own father's interest, and now it had claimed his as well. He knew there would be no turning back for him now, *or ever.*

5 Clues to the Treasure Trail

A COLD, DAMP WIND blew down Cholla Canyon early Monday morning as Gary Cole followed Jim Kermit up the wet slope toward the mouth of the great opening into the Espectros. Jim drew rein and turned to look at Gary. "Sure, I've heard about those old arrastres on the other side of the Espectros, Gary. To my knowledge no one has ever found a trace of a mine in there. You've got to remember this, kid: Since the old Spaniards mined these mountains there have been a lot of changes in the canyons. Flash floods and landslides have done a lot of earth moving in there."

Gary eyed the rugged escarpment of the Espectros, sharp and clear against the rain-washed sky. "I thought we had a real lead for a change, Mr. Kermit," he said.

Jim grinned. "I've lived in these parts for a long time and I've never yet found any float from those old mines. I'm like your grandfather, Gary. Just a rancher at heart, putting my belief into good beef. Your great-grandfather was a dreamer, lad, and I think your father is too. You forget those old lies about lost mines."

"But if there were arrastres built back in those days, they built them to crush ore, and if they crushed ore in them, those mines had to be somewhere near the arrastres."

"Good logic, Gary. But what makes you think you can find the mines if experts have failed? Even your great-grandpa couldn't find that canyon where the mines are supposed to be, and he knew these mountains darned near as well as the Apaches did."

"The mines have to be in there," said Gary stubbornly.

Kermit shrugged. "Well, there was an aerial survey made during the war, and no lost canyons showed, kid. Those aerial cameras show everything, and they didn't show any missing canyons."

Gary looked quickly at him. "Aerial photography! That might do it!"

Jim's eyes hardened. "There you go again! Come on! We've got no time for pipe dreams! I've got strays in these canyons and I want them out of there before dusk! *Vamos!*"

"Is there any way I could get one of those photographs?" persisted Gray.

Jim turned. "Far's I know the negatives were destroyed when a hangar at the air field burned down. I don't know where any of the prints are. Let's go!"

Gary rode on after Jim. He had worked for Jim a number of times. It always seemed to hurt Pete Cole to have to tell Gary there wasn't enough work on the Cole place for him to do. So Gary worked for any of the local ranchers who needed help. Some of them lodged dudes at their places for extra money and had hired Gary as guide into the fringes of the Espectros. Strangely enough, as isolated as the area was, and as mysterious and bloody as its reputation was, the dudes seemed to like it. None of them ever knew they were carefully kept away from the danger zones. More gold had been made from writings about the lost treasures of the Espectros than had been found there.

These writings served to lure the dudes and put gold into the pockets of the ranchers.

Jim turned in his saddle. "Take Cholla Canyon, Gary. I'll follow Split Rock Canyon to where it runs into Cholla and meet you there about noon."

Gary rode slowly toward the looming mouth of Cholla. The Cole place would make an ideal dude ranch. It had a splendid panoramic view of the Espectros. It had a history which had served as the basis for several paperback western novels and countless pulp westerns, none of which had payed a dime into the Cole till. There was a bronze historical marker on the state highway south of the Cole place which told the tale of Chiricahua Springs Ranch. There wasn't any doubt in Gary's mind that the ranch would lure the dudes. Pete Cole could handle that type of work easily enough. It would take money, though, to change the ranch into a dude ranch, and as the situation was now, there wasn't enough money coming in to pay off the loans against it. Jim Kermit was anxious to buy out the Cole place, and he had the money with which to do it.

Gary guided his claybank past a towering growth of saguaros. Maybe Jim Kermit was right. If Great-grandfather Cole had been unable to find the Lost Espectro, it wasn't likely anyone else could find it. What bothered Gary was the fact that history did not lie about the three Melgosa Brothers and their fabulous discovery of gold in the heart of the Espectros in the year 1844. Vigil Melgosa had been killed by the Apaches; Leandro Melgosa had vanished, never to be found again; Marcos Melgosa was said to have sealed off the great mine, leaving a major part of the gold within it, then had fled to Mexico, never to return again. For years after he had left, the Apaches had kept white men from probing into the Espectros. Some white men had entered the mountains despite the Apaches, lured by the promise of the Lost Espectro. None of them had ever returned.

Even today it was said the Apaches still haunted those tangled canyons and inaccessible mesas, and that they knew well enough where the lost mines were hidden. The Apaches believed the Espectros had been the home of ancient gods. Many white people thought it was the Apaches who had committed most of the unsolved murders in the lonely, echoing canyons of the Espectros. There was no proof of this of course; there never was any proof at all as to who perpetrated the murders.

The recent rains had done much damage in Cholla Canyon, sweeping earth into the watercourse at the bottom, piling up brush torn from its roots, moving rocks down the wet slopes. "Flash floods and landslides have done a lot of earth moving in there," Jim Kermit had said. Gary looked up the cold canyon. A thought ran through his mind. *"Flash floods and landslides can also reveal things that have been hidden for many years. . . ."*

He could see no strays as he worked his way up Cholla. Jim Kermit was a hard worker and he expected hard work from his hired hands. To Jim Kermit, losing a stray was like losing a pound of his own flesh. It showed in his ranch, for he was the most prosperous rancher in that area, by dint of perseverance and hard work, or so he always said. *He* took no stock in lost mines.

Cholla Canyon met Split Rock Canyon halfway up the slope of the west side of the Espectros, trending in from the left at an easy angle. Then Split Rock continued on the other, or southerly, side of Cholla Canyon, but here it was called Needle Canyon, for that looming pinnacle of rock dominated the canyon as nothing else did.

Gary rode slowly. He reached the junction and saw no sign of Jim Kermit. There was no use sitting there in the damp waiting for him. Gary rode on. It wasn't until he rode into deeper shadow that he realized he was right below the huge landmark. Closer and closer he rode until he could clearly distinguish features of The Needle he had never seen before—great cracks and splits, crumbling ledges, and eerie-looking holes that might or might not be deep caves. Here and there scattered growths clung to shallow pockets of soil trapped behind ledges.

He forced himself to tear his eyes away from The Needle. Weird thoughts teemed through his mind. He reached for his rifle and then thought better of it. The Cole pride would not allow him to be frightened enough to ride with his rifle in his hand. In any case, if he were shot at, he'd hardly have time to fire back, or even to see who was shooting at him. But the Cole pride would not let him turn back either. There was a job to be done.

It was a wild and forbidding place in which he found himself—a chaotic tangle of brush and rocks, bleached dead wood and splintered boulders. He turned in his saddle to look back down the canyon and found himself looking directly at a deeply chiseled marking on slanted rock ledge. It was an equilateral triangle with a curved line starting from the apex of the triangle and curving downward to the right of the triangle.

His breath caught in his throat. This sudden discovery, after so many months of searching, seemed to stun his senses, but not so much that he did not know what that symbol meant. "Travel around a bend from this symbol," he said aloud.

He looked to his left. A huge outcropping of rock thrust itself into the canyon like the great paw of some primeval beast. Gary slid from the saddle and snatched the reins. He led the claybank toward that outcropping. Forgotten were his father's warning about going past The Needle and also his day's work for Jim Kermit. The sun was at its peak when he found a second symbol, an arrow with a broad head, slanted in the direction he was going. "Trail to treasure or mine; *other signs further on . . .*" Gary said breathlessly.

The canyon beyond was thick with tangled brush and shattered rock, seemingly from a huge landslide of years past, leaving a narrow passageway beyond into shadowed darkness. To his right was yet another narrow canyon curving around to the south in the general direction of The Needle Canyon.

An hour drifted past while Gary hunted for another code symbol. He plowed through catclaw and skirted thick clumps of painful jumping cholla, eagerly scanning rock faces, boulders, and the high crumbling cliffs. No luck. Nothing at all.

He picketed his horse and took the rifle, walking up the side canyon, peering through the brush for symbols. There was nothing to be seen. The Needle towered to his right, and he was quite sure that if he continued on down the canyon he would reach the great canyon below the landmark and easily see the Cole place far below on the level ground. A cold feeling came over him as he realized he must also be close to the general area where he had seen the mysterious spurts of flickering light. He knew now that it was not a figment of his imagination, for hadn't Sue Browne seen the light just the night before?

He continued on, then turned to his left up a steep slope of loose rock. He climbed steadily until the going was a little easier. Now he could see The Needle Canyon as well as Cholla Canyon and the mouth of Split Rock where it joined Cholla. The mysterious, partially blocked canyon was beyond the crest, high above him.

He drove himself on though his legs began to tire a little, and his breath came harshly in his dry throat. Gary stopped and leaned on his rifle for support while he looked upward. There was a dark opening in the naked rock almost at the crest. It was the mouth of a cave that had been well shielded from view below by scattered rock and a screen of brush.

Gary worked his way slowly up to the scattered rock wall and levered a round into his Winchester. He eased himself between two huge boulders and saw the cave mouth. About ten feet within it something was hanging—something that moved a little in the vagrant wind that swept now and then up the canyon. He stared at it, suddenly realizing that it was a sheet of faded canvas, dyed a dun color.

He walked forward slowly and drew back the canvas to peer into the darkened interior of a cave that went far back into the living rock. A damp odor came from the cave, mingled with the smell of old fires and other stale things. He pushed back the thin canvas so that light penetrated into the cave. As he walked into the cave, his left boot struck something that rolled beneath his foot. Gary looked down to see an empty bottle. He stooped and peered into the uninviting darkness. It was almost as though something were far back in there, watching him, waiting for him to come in. He stepped back.

The wind shifted and a faint sound came to Gary—the sound of a man's voice calling out at intervals. Gary took his courage in his hands and walked farther into the cave. To one side was a pile of blankets. Tin cans littered the floor. He bent to look at them. Most of them were without labels but on several of them he saw the labels—they had been cans of Elberta peaches. Beyond the blankets was a crude fireplace filled with ashes and charred wood. He peered into the thick darkness.

The voice was calling again. A sudden fear came over Gary. He ran back to the cave entrance and then stopped in surprise. From where he stood he could see the entire floor of The Needle Canyon and the Cole Ranch far below, and even beyond the ranch to the distant irregular patch against the desert floor that was Cottonwood Wells. Nothing could move on that canyon floor without being seen from the cave entrance, while no one could possibly see that cave from the canyon floor.

Gary stepped beyond the rocks that shielded the cave entrance and looked farther up the slope. He could hear the voice again. He worked his way up the loose and treacherous slope to stand at last on a level area above the cave. He stared in surprise. From where he stood he could see into every canyon about him, while to his right, the east, was a wide tableland stretching into the heart of the Espectros, with the open areas of canyons all about it. From where he stood a man could walk easily to the lips of any of those canyons and see who was in them. From the cave he could see anyone probing about in Cholla Canyon or The Needle Canyon.

The voice called again. Gary turned and looked down into Cholla. A man stood down there with two horses behind him. It was Jim Kermit looking for Gary. Gary turned and slid down the slope. He reached a level place and started across it, only to slip and fall in greasy mud. He shook his head in pain, then saw beyond his muddy boots a set of sharp tracks crossing the mud area. He got to his feet and eyed the strange tracks. They were made by rather small feet, and must have been made sometime that morning after the rain had stopped, for the heavy rains of the day before would have washed them out.

He walked around the muddy area and studied the boot marks. The nail pattern of the left boot heel was clearly marked—a double crescent of nails. The boot heel had either slipped to one side of the boot sole or had been nailed crookedly in place. Beyond the mud, he could see tracks leading down the slope toward Cholla Canyon, only to be lost in the scrub brush halfway down the slope.

Gary slid down the slope to the canyon floor and walked quickly to where Jim Kermit stood, set-faced and with hard eyes. "You figure my strays might be up there, Gary?" the rancher asked coldly.

There was nothing for Gary to say. He was wrong.

"You don't expect me to pay you for today's work, do you, Gary?"

"No, sir."

"What *were* you doing up there?"

"Just looking around."

"Just looking around," mimicked Jim. His voice was heavy with sarcasm. "The Lost Espectro again? You're as big a fool as your great-grandfather was! You take my advice and forget about that fairy tale!" Jim mounted his horse and rode down the canyon. He did not speak again until he was near the first symbol Gary had found, then he turned in his saddle and eyed Gary. "By jiminy," he said. "I'll just bet you saw those phony signs in here: the triangle with the curlicue atop it and that arrow. Was *that* it, Gary? Were you looking for more of *them?*"

There was no need for Gary to answer. His red face gave him away.

Jim Kermit threw back his head. "Hawww!

That's rich! I've seen those things for years, and you were following them! Hawwww! Why even my own daughter Francie knows how phony they are! Wait'll she gets back into high school this fall and tells the other kids about this, Gary! Hawwww!" Jim Kermit shook his head in great amusement and rode on down the canyon. Now and then he would burst into loud laughter.

Gary followed the amused rancher. He might as well go home now. He turned and looked back at the sunlit slopes high above him. If a man was staying in that cave now and then, and had a fire going in there, or perhaps had lighted a cigarette or pipe when the wind flapped the canvas screen, it could be seen down on the desert. But who would stay up there? An uneasiness crept over him. He slapped the claybank on the rump. No luck with the treasure and no pay for that day. His father wouldn't be too happy about that, nor could Gary blame him.

6 The Candyman's Strange Story

It was dusk when Gary arrived home. He had not wanted to face his father. Instead of changing the fortunes of the Coles by finding definite clues to the Lost Espectro he had just made matters worse.

An odd-looking truck was parked beside the windmill. Despite his troubles Gary couldn't help but grin. The truck was the traveling place of business for Fred "Candyman" Platt, as well as the only home he knew. He peddled candy, knickknacks, notions, needles and thread, used tools and books, shotgun shells and rifle cartridges, fishing tackle, and just about every kind of thing a rancher or his family might need between periodic trips to The Wells.

The truck was something like those used by milkmen. The interior was lined with shelves and bins full of Fred's articles of merchandise. There were even shelves on the outside against the walls of the truck, which could be covered by plywood doors when required. Fred also had rigged up a bunk at the front end of the truck, and it was there he slept when on the road. It wasn't an unusual sight to see Fred's truck parked alongside some lonely road and Fred himself seated in a comfortable folding chair smoking his pipe and listening to his radio, miles from any other human being. It was the way he liked it. During the day he lived for his customers; at night and on the weekends he camped by himself, preferring his own company, and finding it good.

Gary's mother turned from the stove as he entered the kitchen after washing up. "You're late, Gary," she said.

There was no use in lying to her. He told her the whole story. He could hear Fred and his father talking in the living room. As long as the "Candyman" was there his father wouldn't make too much of a fuss.

Mrs. Cole took a big meat loaf from the oven.

"I've been against this lost mine business as far back as I can remember. First with your father and then with you. Your grandfather had no interest in the story. Both of you, however, are like Great-grandpa Cole. There seems to be a curse on those who hunt for that mine. Look what happened to your father."

Gary began to set the table. But his mother wasn't through yet.

"Gary," she said, "did you ever know just how your great-grandmother died?"

"Killed by 'Paches," he said. "I know the story by heart."

She shook her head. "You know the story that is on the historical marker. The true one is not told outside of the Cole family. Your great-grandfather left her alone in this very house while he hunted the Lost Espectro. The Apaches knew he wasn't here. They sneaked up and killed three of the Mexicans who were working outside. Your great-grandmother was a brave woman, Gary. She fought from the house and kept them from killing the son who was your grandfather. She died of her wounds.

"It changed your grandfather's life to a certain extent. He raised his son to be a rancher, nothing more. Can you see why?"

"Yet he didn't forget about the Lost Espectro himself. Why else would he have passed his *derrotero* on to his son?"

"I suppose he just couldn't destroy the work of years, useless as it was. Now can you see why the Lost Espectro had a curse upon it, that it brings nothing but tragedy and death to those who hunt it?"

"I guess so," said Gary.

"Will you forget about it as your grandfather did?"

He looked away from her.

"Gary?"

"No, Mother, I can't do that."

For a long moment her soft blue eyes met those hard Cole eyes, legacy of the Cole men, and she knew she couldn't defeat her own son, or his obsession with the Lost Espectro. "Call your father and Mr. Platt," she said quietly.

Fred "Candyman" Platt limped into the room. He smiled at Gary. "Howdy, son! Good to see you! You're getting bigger and bigger!"

Gary smiled. Fred Platt could cheer anyone up. "I see you're limping, Mr. Platt. What happened?"

"Slipped pretty bad. Mebbe I'll tell you the story later. My, that meat loaf smells good, Mis' Cole."

Fred Platt had another function in life as well as that of being a truck peddler. Fred knew all the local news. He didn't gossip, but passed on anything he thought was of importance, if he was sure no one would be hurt in the process. Fred was no carrier of sly tales or malicious slander; he told the news as it had been told to him, no more and no less. At dinner that evening he passed on all the news, but he never stopped eating, for Fred was a good man with a knife and a fork, almost in a class with Tuck Browne if the truth be known.

Fred reached for the potatoes and bumped his ankle against the table leg. He winced in sudden pain. "Hurts worse than ever," he said. "Taped it up after putting liniment on it. Could hardly get in and out of the ol' truck today. Shifting gears was a hardship I tell you."

"How did you hurt it?" asked Mrs. Cole.

"You know how hard it rained yesterday evening? Well early this morning I stepped out'a the truck and slipped on some 'dobe mud. Got pretty fine bones, Mis' Cole. Don't take much to hurt 'em."

"Maybe you'd better lay off a day or two," she said.

His unusually dark blue eyes seemed to flash. "I got customers to service, Mis' Cole!"

"That takes care of that," said Pete Cole dryly. "'Neither snow nor rain nor heat nor gloom of night stays these couriers from the swift completion of their appointed rounds.'"

The Candyman looked quickly at Pete. "Nice," he said. "What is it?"

Pete smiled. "Herodotus, the Greek historian, wrote that about the Persian postal system of 500 B.C. It's a quotation used to describe the present-day performance of our postmen."

Fred passed a hand over his thinning blond hair. "Well, I do my job. Folks depend on the ol' Candyman. Woman might want some baking powder, or thread, or mebbe a corn plaster. Who *else* would get it to her?"

"He's only kidding you, Candyman," said Lucille Cole.

The peddler again filled his plate. "Well, as much as I hate to think about it, I got to keep going all week. This is the week I go plumb around to the north side of the Espectros."

"Too bad Gary is working for Jim Kermit," said Pete. "He can drive as well as any man."

Gary looked quickly at his mother. She nodded. "So happens, Mr. Platt, that Jim Kermit let me go today," said Gary. "I'd like to drive for you this week."

"Capital!" said the peddler. "Won't be easy! Hard work! Long hours! Moving all the time! You won't get tired driving?"

"I never get tired of driving, Mr. Platt."

"You're young. It's rough country to the north."

"Just don't let him wander off into the mountains, Candyman," said Pete Cole, half in earnest and half in fun.

Fred's eyes narrowed. "Why would he do that?" He brightened suddenly. "The Lost Espectro! I might have known! Listen, boy, that ain't nothing but a fairy tale! If there *was* such a mine, which I *doubt,* all traces of it would have vanished long ago. You won't get anywhere dreaming about those lost mines, kid. Hard work is the formula for success! Look at me! Just a grade school education and I already got my own business! Well established! Well thought of! Welcome anywhere as a solid, respected citizen of the community!" Fred sawed off another thick slice of meat loaf. "I pass them mountains every week," he continued. "Sure, I look at 'em and wonder if there ever was such a bonanza as the Lost Espectro, but I got enough sense to know my fortune is in my ol' truck. I *look* at them mountains, Gary, but I never go into them canyons I tell you! Too many queer things happening in there to suit the Candyman!

Lost treasures don't mean that much to me. There are plenty of other things to be interested in. Money ain't everything, boy!"

Even Lucille Cole had to hide a smile. They all knew that Fred Platt would carry his laden truck on his back up to the top of The Needle if he thought there was a customer on that aerie. It was an obsession with Fred to serve his customers, and it was certainly not to his discredit.

Pete Cole reached for the coffeepot. "I heard that Asesino was looking for some cartridge-reloading equipment for that old rifle of his," he said casually.

"Well so happens I got a set of secondhand Lyman reloading gear," said Fred quickly. He hesitated and looked quizzically at Pete. "Did you say '*Asesino*'?"

Pete grinned. "I was only joshing you, Candyman."

"That ain't a thing to josh about, Pete! No offense to you, but some people might want to know how you found out."

"About the reloading equipment?" asked Pete in delight. He burst into laughter. "You don't believe I actually heard that, do you?"

"Pete is only teasing you, Candyman," said Lucille.

The peddler turned slowly to look at her. "I don't like being teased about *him*," he said. He glanced quickly toward the closest window as though someone might be eavesdropping.

"The man is long dead," said Pete seriously.

"No," said the peddler. "Asesino is still alive."

"You've talked to him lately?" asked Pete. "Sold him a packet of needles? Come now, Candyman!"

Fred's face was pale and taut. "There have been times I know I've been watched—the times when I camped too close to the canyon mouths. Once or twice I saw someone moving about on the canyon rims. I'm pretty sure it was him, Pete."

There was a skeptical look on Pete Cole's face. "Come off it, Fred," he said. "Don't start wild stories about him. There are people who believe he is still alive, you know."

Fred leaned closer to Pete. "I knew him years ago," he said quietly. "I couldn't be mistaken."

"Over thirty years ago?" echoed Lucille Cole. "Do you really think you'd know him after all those years?"

Fred straightened up. "Well, I might as well tell you. I think I seen him no later than yesterday morning!"

"Where?" asked Pete.

"I was camped east of the mountains. Not too

far from that plugged up canyon there. I had parked my truck close under a cliff so as to get out of the sun. That was late Saturday afternoon. Had a quiet night. Didn't do much Sunday morning except laze around and look for geodes and the like. I get a good price for them from rock hounds. I wandered quite a ways from the truck, leaving it open to air out. Well, I was getting tired, so I started back. I wasn't one hundred yards from the truck when I seen him. . . ."

Gary felt the cold creeping of fear over his body. He remembered all too well his own feelings when he was in a canyon and thought he was being watched.

"He was standing by the rear of the truck as calm as you please, eatin' something out of a can. I was scairt I tell you! I turned to run and kicked a rock lying there. I looked back. He was standing there looking right at me. . . .

Somewhere out in the stillness of the desert night a coyote howled softly. Lucille Cole shivered a little.

"His eyes was like coals of fire!" said Fred in a louder voice. "He was ragged and dirty but he moved like a cat! His rifle was leaning against a rock! He run for it, and I run the other way! Then I fell down, and when I had the nerve to look back, he was gone. Nothing on that empty ground but my old truck! He had vanished like a ghost!"

Gary glanced at his father. Pete seemed intent on what Fred had been saying. The man wasn't known to be a liar. The fact was that no man in Gary's knowledge and in that of his father as well had actually claimed to have *seen* Asesino in the past ten or fifteen years, although there were plenty of rumors that he *had* been seen, but no one ever seemed to know *who* had seen him. If Fred's story was true then here was concrete evidence that the feared outlaw was still alive.

Fred hitched his chair closer to the table and refilled his coffee cup. "When I got to the truck I found three empty cans lying there."

"What had he been eating?" asked Lucille.

Fred looked up with an odd little smile. "Peaches! Not them little cans! The big ones! Three whole cans of Elberta peaches, Mis' Cole. That was another reason I was sure it was him."

Gary had become tense. He stared at the talkative peddler. Elberta peaches! Some of the cans in the mysterious cave he had entered that very day had once been filled with the luscious fruit. "Why did that convince you it was really him, Mr. Platt?" asked Gary quietly.

The peddler smiled knowingly. "I said I had

known him years ago. If there was one thing Asesino loved, besides killing that is, it was Elberta peaches! Don't ask me why." He smiled again. "It's a cinch he ain't buying his peaches up in the Espectros!"

"What did he really look like?" asked Mrs. Cole.

"Like a ghost! An *espectro!* Cries out like one too."

"Cries out?" asked Gary quickly. "How?"

"Well, I can't make it sound exactly like he does it, but it's some thing like this." Fred threw back his head, cupped his hands about his mouth, and gave voice to a wailing, eerie cry; a mournful thing, thin and haunting.

Gary paled. It was much like the sound he and Tuck had heard that night in the canyon.

"Elberta peaches," said Pete. He shook his head. "Anything else missing?"

"Yeh. A box of cartridges. Kind'a odd caliber too: .50/110 they was. I used to carry them for Old Man Mills some years ago. He never came into town so I carried them as a sort of service for him. Well, when he died, his son came out from Albuquerque, took one look around, then put the place up for sale or lease and went right back to Albuquerque! Guess he either left the old rifle in the place or else took it with him. Well, I carried that box around such a long time I was almost glad to get rid of 'em. Ain't many rifles that caliber still being used."

Pete nodded. "It is an odd caliber, though not quite as rare as you'd think it would be. Came out in the Winchester Model 1886 repeater. Probably one of the smoothest level action rifles ever manufactured. It was usually a heavy-caliber gun in .45/70, .38/56, .40/82, and .45/90 calibers. The .50/110 was the largest of them."

"Say," said Fred admiringly. "That's all right!"

Gary smiled proudly. "Dad is a gun crank. Anything you want to know about guns you just ask him."

"It was a .50/110 slug that killed my horse and dumped me down to the bottom of a canyon," said Pete quietly. "I ought to know it."

"Sure could make a hole in a man," said Gary.

Fred looked quickly at Gary. "What do you mean?"

Gary looked at his father. "Can I show Fred that skull I found?"

Pete Cole smiled, and then looked at his wife. "Not in here, Gary."

"I'll serve coffee and cake in the living room," said Mrs. Cole hastily.

Later, as Fred Platt examined the bullet-punctured skull he nodded. "Large-caliber slug all right."

"You remember those two prospectors who went into the Espectros about twelve years ago, Fred?" asked Pete.

"Yeh. They found one of 'em with a bullet hole in the back of his head. They never did find the other one."

Pete leaned forward and tapped the skull. "This is quite possibly the skull of the one they never found. Tell him the story, Gary."

Gary told the story of finding the skeleton in the canyon of the arrastres. "There was a belt buckle with the skeleton," he continued. "Initials J. B. "

"I think you're right, Pete," said Fred. "The one they found dead in the camp was a man named Carl Schuster. His partner was a man named John Bellina. It all ties in."

"Gary plans to take the relics into town and have them turned over to Sheriff Gates," said Pete.

Fred hefted the skull. "I wouldn't."

"Why not?" asked Gary.

Fred looked about as though someone might again be eavesdropping. "They haven't been able to find Carl Schuster's killer in twelve years, have they? No! And they won't either. Likely them fellas was hot on the trail of the Lost Espectro. They *knew* too much. They was killed because they knew too much, and for no other reason. Now, I think the place where Gary found this skeleton and them arrastres is mighty close to the Lost Espectro. This is a great lead, Gary. I ain't interested naturally. All the money in Arizona wouldn't get *me* into the Espectros to look for haunted treasure, and besides, after seeing Asesino yesterday, I ain't ever going near them canyons again!"

"So?" said Pete. "But why not tell the Sheriff?"

Fred smiled almost as though he were explaining something to a child. "If any man has the right to the Lost Espectro it's you, Pete, and Gary here too. Supposing the Sheriff does get this stuff? He won't likely know any more than they did twelve years ago. But these clues won't be kept secret if the Sheriff gets hold of them. It'll be in the papers and on the radio and TV, I'll bet. In a week them mountains will be crawling with people looking for the Lost Espectro. This time one of them just might be lucky. No, Pete, you keep this to yourself. I won't talk. Seems like Gary has really stumbled onto something this time. Never say die, eh, boy?"

"I don't want him wandering around in there," said Pete.

Fred smiled. "He's got the Cole blood, ain't he?" He handed Pete the skull. "Anyway I'll keep him so busy the rest of this week he won't have time to look for any lost mine. Come to think of it, I need a partner. Been thinking of expanding. Two trucks. Twice as much business. Need a young fella with energy and ideas. What do you say, Gary?"

Gary tried to make his answering smile look realistic, but he was shuddering inwardly. Some local wag would start calling him "Junior, the Candyman" or something equally horrible.

Fred got up. "I'll sleep in my truck tonight. Put that skull under your pillow, Gary. Might tell you the secret of the Lost Espectro in the dark of the moon. Hawww! Best get to bed, Gary. We leave at dawn."

"Cheerful fellow," said Pete after Fred left. He filled his pipe and lighted it. He eyed Gary over the flare of the match. "Fred might be right at that. Let's keep this skull business to ourselves, for a time at least."

"Does that mean I can keep on looking for the Lost Espectro?"

Pete puffed at his pipe. "I don't really know how

I can stop you," he said. He smiled ruefully. "Almost wish I could go with you. I wonder if he really *did* see Asesino?"

"*Quien sabe?*" said Gary.

The coyote howled again. Closer to the house this time. Gary eyed the grinning skull. It was a fact that Apaches could imitate the cries of animals and birds almost to perfection. Asesino had been part Apache.

7 The Lone Apache

DURING THE THREE DAYS Gary drove for Fred "Candyman" Platt, he learned things about the western and northern approaches to the Espectros he had never known before. The northern side of the mountains was almost a land apart from that which he had known around his father's ranch. Not far from it was the border of the Apache Reservation. The last stop on Fred Platt's lengthy and lonely northern route was the old Mills Ranch, a place that had been built some years after Jim Cole had established his Chiricahua Springs Ranch. It had been burned out a number of times, and once there had been a massacre there from which there had been no survivors.

The truck ground along in low gear through the desert sands. Gary wondered how Fred could possibly make any sort of a profit by selling a packet of needles or a bag of hard candy in such a remote part of the Espectro Mountain country. Their goal showed in a spray of dusty green against the dun of the Espectro foothills, a sure sign of water in the almost waterless land. Behind a screen of trees were the ranch buildings. A dog barked as Gary drove up and stopped the truck at the gate.

A man rounded the corner of a shed and walked easily toward the truck. He was not tall but his chest was deep and broad, and his slim hips were the mark of the horseman. "Hiya, Candyman!" he called. "Come on in!"

"Hello, Jerry! Hot, ain't it?"

The man smiled, revealing even white teeth. Gary studied him. He had seen many Apaches in his lifetime, and he knew now he was looking at one of the pure quill. The man seemed to be staring right through Gary. "You look familiar," he said easily.

Fred nodded. "This is Gary Cole, Jerry. Gary, this is Jerry Black. Black is short for Black Eagle, ain't it, Jerry?"

"Something like that," agreed the Apache. He held out a hand to Gary. "Your dad ever tell you about me, kid?"

"Not that I know of," said Gary.

"Maybe you'd know me better by the name they called me in the Marine outfit I served in with your dad. Geronimo!"

Gary grinned. "Sure!" he said. "You were with him all through the war!"

"How's your dad?"

"Not too well, Jerry."

"War wound still bothering him?"

"Yes, but it was that fall some years ago that did the worst damage."

A fleeting change came over the dark face. "They ever find out who shot at him?"

"Some folks think it was Asesino," said Fred.

Jerry grinned and waved a hand. "Not that old fairly tale again! Asesino is dead. Long gone!"

"Are you sure about that, Jerry?" asked Fred.

"Why, it's been years since anyone has seen him!"

Fred looked at Gary. He was behind the Apache. The peddler shook his head. Gary looked up at the shimmering Espectros, vague and unreal in the shifting light. "I've heard stories he's still up there."

Jerry shoved back his hat and took out a sack of

Bull Durham. He deftly rolled a cigarette and lighted it. His dark eyes studied Gary through the smoke. "I go into those mountains all the time, kid. When I got out of college I started exploring in there. That was twelve years ago. I haven't seen Asesino or anyone like him in there. Sure the man *did* exist. Sure, he was an outlaw and a killer. But folks have built up a legend about him like they did about Billy the Kid and Wyatt Earp, making him do things he never did."

Gary took a chance. "I thought you Apaches shunned the Espectros because of old tribal taboos and so on."

Again the fleeting look passed over Jerry's face. "That's cornball stuff for the old rimrock 'Paches, kid. Four years in the Marines and four years in college knocked all that hokey stuff out of me, I tell you!"

"Jerry gets a little bitter sometimes, kid," Fred said. "Seems like it ain't easy for a college-educated Apache to get a good job around here."

Jerry grunted. "They still think I'd scalp anyone who disagreed with me. Well, come on in. I have some cold drinks in the refrigerator." He walked quickly to the house.

Fred limped alongside Gary, holding onto his shoulder. "Jerry leases the Mills place. Doesn't run cattle or anything though. He's writing a book or something. Spends a lot of time hunting for relics in the mountains. That's why I come out here. Don't say anything about me seeing Asesino."

Gary's eyes widened as he saw the things Jerry had brought out of the mountains. They were placed on a big table in the shaded living room—pottery, arrowheads, basketry, husk matting, and other odds and ends. Hung on the walls were rusted spurs, bits, old guns, bridles, and other relics.

Jerry brought in a tray with glasses and a sweating pitcher filled with tinkling ice and ginger ale. "What do you think of my collection?" he asked.

"Terrific! Museum pieces some of them."

"Hardly that, Gary," said the Apache dryly. "Fred peddles some of the stuff for me."

"Now you know why I come all the way out here to this suburb of Hades," grumbled Fred.

"And this is how you make your living, Jerry?" asked Gary.

Jerry nodded. "It keeps me going while I do research on my book about the Espectro Mountain country."

"It's supposed to be against the law to loot ruins," blurted out Gary without thinking. He was guilty of the same thing himself.

Jerry's dark eyes hardened. "Maybe it is," he said in a low voice, "but the state doesn't seem much concerned about how I live. If I don't dig out those relics to make a fast buck now and then I'd go hungry. Besides, who else would go that deep into those canyons? Remember Asesino, kid! Remember the men with the bullet holes in their skulls! Remember the mysterious marksman of death who keeps inquisitive strangers out of the inner canyons!"

"It ain't funny," said Fred sourly. "Remember it was Gary's pa who got shot in there. By God's grace he come out alive."

Jerry rested a hand on Gary's shoulder. "I'm sorry," he said. "I get a little bitter at times. Does your father still talk about the Lost Espectro, kid? It used to be his chief topic of conversation overseas."

"I just told him the other night that he and Gary had the best right to the Lost Espectro."

Jerry's eyes flicked up. "*No* man has a right to the Lost Espectro."

Fred tinkled the ice in his glass. "Oh, I've heard tell you 'Paches know exactly where it is but you won't talk. How about that, Jerry?"

Jerry did not speak. He waved a hand toward

the relics on the table. "How much of this junk do you want, Candyman?"

Fred winked at Gary. "You didn't answer my question, Jerry."

The Apache turned slowly. "Do you want this stuff or not, Fred?"

Gary wandered over to look at the items hanging on the wall. He noticed with a start that there were several mule shoes with flared ends identical to those he and his companions had found near the arrastres. Jerry looked at him. "Ever see mule shoes like those, kid?" he asked.

"No," lied Gary.

"Spanish style. They still make them that way in Mexico."

"You didn't find these in an old cliff dwelling," said Gary.

"No. Over on the southeast side of the Espectros there is a blind canyon with some old arrastres in it. I found those shoes around there."

"Interesting," said Gary over his shoulder. "You find anything else in there?"

"Such as?"

"Lost mines?"

There was a moment's hesitation, and then Jerry spoke. "I wouldn't know," he said quietly. "I'm not interested in them as such. There are less dangerous things in there."

"Why dangerous?" prodded Gary.

"All old mines are dangerous. In the canyon where I found those mule shoes there is always danger of falling rocks because of the rock formations in it. A man could easily get killed in there."

"Yeh," said Fred dryly. "In more ways than one. Gary, take this stuff out into the truck and make sure it's packed right. I don't want any of it broken."

Gary carried the box to the truck and stowed it away. He walked to the windmill and scooped up some water from the trough to wash his sweaty face. As he turned away he saw something brassy-bright lying beside one of the legs of the windmill. He picked up a large brass cartridge and turned it to see the base. It was marked W.R.A. Co. .50/110 Ex. "Winchester Repeating Arms Company," he translated, "Caliber .50/110 Express Cartridge." He swiftly palmed the brass hull and slipped it into his Levi's pocket as Fred and Jerry walked toward the truck.

Fred limped to the truck. Sweat dewed his red face. "I hate to call it quits," he moaned, "but we'd better head back home, Gary. This heat and my ankle are killing me." Gary helped him into the truck. Jerry beckoned to Gary and walked toward the windmill. Gary felt a twinge of fear. Had Jerry seen him pick up that cartridge case?

Jerry smiled. "Tell your dad I'll be by the ranch to see him one of these days. How is it going?"

"Pretty tough, Jerry. He has his pension and I work when I can, but it isn't enough to keep the ranch, I'm afraid."

"As bad as all that?"

Gary nodded.

Jerry glanced toward the shimmering mountains. "And with all that gold supposed to be hidden in there so close to your place."

"Then you really believe in the Lost Espectro?"

"Of course."

"And not Asesino?"

Jerry began to roll another cigarette. "I'll bet he's long dead, kid. You keep looking for the mine. It's in there all right. You weren't too far from it the other day."

Gary looked quickly at him. How had he known they had been looking in the canyon of the arrastres?

Jerry lighted the cigarette. He blew a smoke ring. "Dangerous in there, kid. Lot of falling rock." The dark eyes studied Gary.

If Jerry had been in there he must have seen

that skeleton and the bullet-punctured skull as well. The hole in the skull had been a big one. A .50/110 bullet might have made such a hole. It seemed to Gary that the empty hull in his pocket was burning against his flesh.

"You happen to see the skeleton and the skull with the bullet hole in it?" asked Jerry casually.

Gary nodded. His throat tasted like brass.

Jerry blew a smoke ring and stabbed a finger through it. "You going to tell the Sheriff about it?" he asked.

"Why didn't you if you knew it was in there?" asked Gary boldly.

Jerry smiled. "Remember I'm an *Apache*, kid. Ignorant and superstitious despite my college degree. Apaches won't stay near the dead. It's taboo. Like you White-Eyes say, we 'Paches steer clear of the Espectros. There are things in there we do not like. The undead haunt these mountains. Bu, the Owl, calls at night in the voices of the restless spirits of the dead." The dark eyes studied Gary.

Jerry looked again at the mountains. "I know one thing, kid. If you ever find that old *derrotero* your great-grandfather made, you might just get a lead on the Lost Espectro."

"No one knows where it is."

"If you ever find it, keep it to yourself. There are

men around these mountains who'd do anything to get their hands on it. Kill even . . ."

"Yeh," said Gary weakly.

"You believe that, don't you?"

Gary nodded.

"You ever see any of those old Spanish mining symbols in the canyons?"

"Yes. In Cholla Canyon. Jim Kermit said they were phonies."

"He did? Kermit said that?"

"Yes."

Jerry smiled knowingly. "Well, he might *say* so, but Jim Kermit can keep his mouth shut when it comes to making a fast buck. You ever see Jim Kermit need money? The rest of the ranchers around here are always borrowing money, but not Jim. Jim always has a buck."

"Gary!" called Fred from the truck. "You aim to let me roast in here?"

"Go ahead, kid," said Jerry. "Keep hunting for the mine. Something tells me you might be the lucky one."

Gary shrugged. All the way to the truck he could feel those dark eyes boring into his back.

When the truck reached the road Fred glanced at Gary. "Jerry is a bitter man. I think he knows a lot more about those mountains than he lets on.

'Course I can't see an *Indian* getting the rights *we* got, but don't tell him I said that."

"He's a citizen, isn't he? He fought in the war. He was in my father's outfit."

"Sho! What'd he do?"

"Seems to me my father told me once he was a sniper." Then a cold feeling came over Gary. Jerry *had* been a sniper, a dead shot with a rifle in the jungles of the Pacific Islands. He had made a record for himself in that deadly game. Asesino had also been handy with a rifle. Maybe Asesino was dead, but there was nothing to stop Jerry from taking up the trade of the outlaw. Maybe it was Jerry that Fred Platt had seen last Sunday. Maybe Jerry wanted to keep the legend of Asesino alive so that men would fear the Espectros. Killing was no novelty to Jerry Black.

Fred eased his leg. "I'm taking off tomorrow, Gary. I'll pay you anyway. Friday, Saturday, and Sunday ought'a be enough rest for this game leg of mine."

"You don't have to pay me for Friday, Mr. Platt."

"Sho! You did a good job, kid. Besides, it was nice having company. I learned a lot listening to you, Gary. Fella gets lonesome out in these places."

Gary smiled. Fred Platt had a name for being close with a buck, but Gary had always thought he kept up that pretense so people wouldn't know how really softhearted he was.

Gary glanced at the Espectros. He and Tuck would have three full days to continue their search. This time Gary was bound and determined they would come out of there with some definite conclusion about the Lost Espectro.

8 Search for the Derrotero

A LONE LUGUBRIOUS FIGURE was perched on the fence in front of the Cole house when Gary drove up in the truck. Tucker C. Browne looked like a dejected stork sitting there. He brightened when he saw Gary. "What are you doing here?" he asked.

Gary grinned. "Mr. Platt isn't running his route tomorrow, so he gave me the day off with pay, Tuck."

Gary got out of the truck. He looked back at Fred Platt. "Are you sure you can drive all right, Mr. Platt?"

The peddler nodded. "So long as I don't have

to drive too much. I got some business in The Wells and other places I can take care of without too much driving. Say hello to your mother and father, Gary."

"They ain't here," Tuck said, inelegantly. "That's why I'm here. Your father's back started bothering him, and your mother had to drive him to the V. A. Hospital in Tucson. They left early this morning. They won't be back until Sunday evening if they don't keep your father there, Gary. Your mother asked me to come out and stay at the place until you got back. Between you and me I was hoping you'd come back today or tonight. I wasn't looking forward to staying here alone tonight."

"Afraid of Asesino?" asked Fred. He grinned.

Tuck shrugged. "I never like being around the Espectros alone, Mr. Platt. Besides, lots of people think this place is haunted too. There were so many killings around here in the old days."

"Hokey," said Gary.

Fred eased his way into the driver's seat. "Oh, I don't know," he said quietly. "Lots of things we don't know about haunts and suchlike. Once in a while I see things out in the desert at night I ain't sure about."

"Like Asesino?" asked Tuck in delight. "Hawww!"

"Like Asesino," agreed Fred. He glanced quickly at Gary. "You can tell him when I leave, Gary."

Gary nodded. "He won't be so cocky then."

Fred looked toward the house. "Well, now you've got plenty of time to search for the Lost Espectro, haven't you?"

"That's the idea," said Tuck brightly.

"Too bad that ol' *derrotero* vanished," said the peddler. "I always figured one of two things could have happened to it. It was either stolen when your folks wasn't around here, Gary, or it's still here some place."

"Yeh," said Gary dryly. "But where? We've looked all over the house, outbuildings, fence post holes, and even around the Springs. No luck. Not even a clue."

"Keep looking," said Fred. "Tuck, you go into the back of the truck and help yourself to a box of candy bars. You look peaked."

Tuck obeyed with a speed a little short of light. He grinned as he came to the front of the truck. "Thanks a lot, Mr. Platt."

"Forget it. I was a growing boy myself once. Keep looking for that *derrotero,* boys. You're bound to find it."

"I got some ideas on that myself," said Tuck.

Fred started the truck and drove off. Tuck held

out the candy box to Gary. "Help yourself, *amigo.* On the house."

Gary took a bar and peeled it, but his eyes were on the hazy Espectros. "We've got three days," he said thoughtfully. "When do you have to be home?"

"Doesn't matter," said Tuck around the last half of his first bar. "My folks know I'm out here. I usually am weekends anyway. Worked all week long at Bennie's Barbecue, so I got some spending loot."

"I'll bet Bennie lost on the deal," said Gary.

Tuck peeled his second bar. "Well I got to admit he told me to take it easy on the french fries."

"Let's get some chow," said Gary. "I have a few things I want to tell you."

They ate in the kitchen while Gary told Tuck of his experiences and particularly of Jerry Black.

Tuck constructed his third ham sandwich. "This thing gets more confusing every time we talk it over. I always wondered why Jim Kermit never seemed to be interested in the Lost Espectro, being the man with a buck that he is. Maybe Jerry Black is right at that. Jim just might claim those markings were phonies to keep nosy people away from Cholla Canyon."

"On the other hand," said Gary, "maybe Jerry

is making Jim look suspicious to keep nosy people from wondering what he's doing all the time up in the mountains."

"Yeh," said Tuck around a mouthful of bread and ham. "But somehow I want to believe in those two symbols you found in Cholla."

"They look real enough to me."

Tuck swallowed hard. "But I've always heard that Cholla is a dead end somewhere in the Espectros."

Gary finished his sandwich and leaned back in his chair. "It looked to me like there had been a landslide in there. There's something beyond that slide, Tuck."

"Yeh, like Asesino maybe. You really think Fred saw him?"

"*Quien sabe?* He saw *somebody*—somebody that liked Elberta peaches. Like the somebody who stays in that cave now and then. Tuck, I tell you, those boot prints I saw were fresh!"

"Maybe Jim Kermit was up there ahead of you."

"I was at his place before dawn, Tuck. I was with him until we entered the canyons and there wasn't any place he could have gotten ahead of me. No, those boot prints were made by someone else. Maybe by the person who has been staying in that cave."

"Like Jerry maybe?"

Gary shrugged. "He keeps pretty much to himself. No one seems to know much about him, even Fred Platt, and Fred seems to know something about everybody."

Tuck nodded. "But this Jerry keeps coming back to my mind, *amigo.* I remember him all right. Looks a hole right through you. Man, he's a natural suspect for my money."

"That's just it, Tuck! He's just too much of a natural! Asesino was part Apache; Jerry is full-blooded. Asesino really knew those mountains; so does Jerry. Asesino was a dead shot; Jerry was a sniper in the Marines. Asesino was a lone wolf; Jerry likes to stay by himself. Asesino didn't seem to be much concerned about the superstitions the Apaches attach to the Espectros; Jerry doesn't seem much concerned either. Asesino was bitter against the white man; Jerry is bitter as well. Asesino quite likely carried a .50/110 caliber Winchester and I found an empty .50/110 hull at Jerry's place."

"Sounds like a lot of circumstantial evidence," said Tuck wisely. He began to prepare a fourth sandwich, cutting into the ham with the skill of a surgeon. "It's just too pat. Besides, and don't ask me why, I happen to like Jerry Black."

"Me too," agreed Gary.

"You keep talking about Asesino in the past tense," said Tuck. "Why? Maybe Fred Platt really saw him."

"Fred Platt isn't a liar, Tuck. He actually knew Asesino years ago. So, Asesino swipes a box of .50/110 caliber cartridges from Fred's truck and three cans of Elbertas. Fred said Asesino loved Elbertas."

"Phooey," said Tuck. He mustarded, ketch-upped, lettuced and mayonnaised his sandwich. "Big deal! I love Elbertas! You like 'em! Why even Sue eats them like popcorn! Lije Purtis would walk ten miles to get a can of Elbertas." Tuck's voice died away and his eyes widened. "Lije Purtis!" he added in an odd voice.

"The man who doesn't know how to use a gun," said Gary.

"At a distance a man who looked as ragged and dirty as Lije could sure look like he'd been in the mountains a long time. Maybe Fred got mixed up. He was scared you said, and he was quite a ways from the truck."

"I know two characters in this house who are more mixed up than he is," said Gary dryly.

"Have you thought any more about that crazy *derrotero*?"

"I think about it all the time," said Gary. "Like Fred said, it was either stolen when my folks weren't around or it's still here. It just has to be one or the other!"

"Big help," said Tuck. "Where'd we leave those candy bars?"

Gary left Tuck and walked into the living room. It was getting dark outside. He sat down in his father's big chair, a legacy of Grandfather Cole's. Gary closed his eyes. His head ached with thinking about that lost *derrotero. If* it was hidden in the house, it surely must have been well hidden; Gary and his father had once conducted a systematic search for it, and Gary's mother had even helped them. It had been no use.

Yet something rankled at the back of his mind. He had been an infant when the *derrotero* vanished. It had been about the time his mother decided to move into town to stay with her widowed father who hadn't been feeling too well. With Pete Cole in the hospital, the Cole Ranch was a right lonely place for a young mother and a baby boy.

Gary could hear Tuck calling to Lobo to feed him the ham bone. The big dog barked as he raced toward the back porch of the ranch house. Then Gary could hear Tuck in deep conversation with the dog. Tuck liked that. It let him do all the talking. He was telling the dog he'd have to work for the bone.

"Nineteen forty-six," said Gary aloud. He started and sat up. Why had he said that date?

He could hear Lobo chasing Tuck around the house and the bloodcurdling cries of the lean one were enough to send a chill down the spine of Asesino.

He stood up and paced back and forth. "I was only a baby then. That was the year my mother took me to stay at The Wells." He stared at the wall and smashed a fist into his other palm. He certainly could not remember staying with his grandfather there. Grandfather Hart, the retired high school principal of Cottonwood Wells Union High School, had died the first year Gary had started school. Gary could remember him. He always seemed to have a pipe in one hand and a book in the other. Where Great-grandfather Cole had been a man who had probed into the mysterious Espectros to make his precious *derrotero* and to find traces of the old Spanish and Mexican miners by tracking them down, Grandfather Hart had been strictly an armchair explorer, although his interest in lost treasures and in the

Espectro was every bit as keen as that of Great-grandfather Cole's.

There was a tremendous crashing noise outside and the sound of splashing water while Lobo barked in delight. Gary walked to the window. A pair of skinny legs protruded from the water trough and then Tuck Browne's lean face showed above the edge of the trough. He climbed out, sluicing water from every stitch of his clothing. He limped toward the house. Lobo barked again. Tuck turned. "You did that on purpose, Lobo," he said, and tossed him the wet ham bone.

The Hart house, now unoccupied, still stood on a side street in The Wells. It had been left to Gary's mother and she had kept it, always thinking that when the day came for the ranch to be sold, the family could move into the Hart house. The house had been rented several times but never for very long. There were more modern rentals in the newer part of The Wells.

"Tuck," said Gary.

The lean one was wringing out his trousers. "Yeh?" he said in soppy disgust.

"We're going to take a ride!"

"To where?"

"My grandfather's old house in The Wells."

"Nothing there," said Tuck.

"I have a feeling we've been looking in the wrong place for the *derrotero,* Tuck! The *derrotero* vanished about 1946; in 1946 my father was still in the hospital, and my mother and I were staying with Grandfather Hart."

Tuck stopped wringing. "By jiminy!" he said quietly. "Grandfather Hart was loco about such things. You think maybe the chart was taken there and forgotten?"

"I'll take a chance that it might be there."

"Keno! Let me change my clothes!"

Gary got the jeep and was waiting for Tuck. He ordered Lobo to stay behind and drove out onto the darkening road. There was an intense eagerness within him. Nothing had been changed in the old house. Every now and then Gary would go into town and clean up the grounds of the place, cut the lawns, and sometimes, accompanied by Tuck, he'd stay the night in the gloomy old house. Not once had he ever considered that the *derrotero* might be hidden there.

It was quite dark when they pulled up in front of the old house, dreaming on its quiet side street. Gary unlocked the double front door and it creaked open.

"Always thought this place was haunted," said Tuck.

"You think every place is haunted," said Gary. "I'll go in alone if you're chicken."

"Who me? Fearless Browne? 'Lead on, MacDuff!' "

The street lamp shone through the stained glass at the top of the big door and made an eerie reddish pattern on the faded wallpaper. Gary quickly led the way up the wide creaking stairs. "I figure we'd better hunt in the library," he said. "That's where Grandpa Hart spent most of his time."

The library was in the front of the house, across the hall from the huge master bedroom. Gary walked into the dim room faintly lighted by the street lamp. He lighted an oil lamp and turned to look at the serried ranks of bookshelves that entirely lined the big room. "I've heard of papers being hidden in hollowed out books," he said.

"Sounds like a story from Poe," said Tuck. "Hollowed out books! Hoooooey!"

"You got any better ideas?"

"Let's look for hollowed out books."

An hour passed while the two boys took down one book at a time and examined it. Their hands were black with dust, and dust floated about the room and swirled about the draft of hot air rising from the lamp on the table.

"Man," said Tuck in grudging admiration, "your grandpap was sure a readin' man."

Gary nodded. He had reached the end of one row of shelves, and he reached for the first book in the next row. His hand stopped part way and he stared at the row of books.

"What is it, Gary?" asked Tuck.

"Look, Tuck," said Gary. "Every book on these shelves is marked with fingerprints."

Tuck eyed the books. "Yeh," he said. "When was the last time any of your family were in here?"

"Early last spring—and we didn't dust the books as I recall."

Tuck whistled softly. "Someone was pawing around in here then," he said. He raised the lamp. "Look, Gary. That whole wall of books back there have been handled too. Lookit the finger marks on 'em!"

A cold feeling came over Gary. Someone had been in there then. Someone who might have gotten the same idea that had occurred to Gary.

"Ghosts," said Tuck.

"Ghost don't leave fingerprints!" snapped Gary.

"Take it easy! I was only joking, *amigo.*"

Gary shook his head. He was getting discouraged. Maybe this idea was a bust too. Everything connected with the story of the Lost Espectro seemed to be a bust.

Tuck walked to the end shelf, close to the door. Here the books still had their coating of dust. He grinned. "Just supposing that clod who was looking through these books stopped a little short of finding the *derrotero?*" he asked.

"Those holes in your thick head make your voice sound funnier than usual."

Tuck reached up and withdrew a heavy volume. He hefted it. "Seems lighter than it should be," he said. He lifted the front cover and looked down at the book. For a moment his face was set and frozen. "Gary," he said in a hoarse voice.

"Don't tell me you've found it?" cracked Gary. He started to reach for another book.

"Gary!"

Gary turned quickly. Tuck handed him the thick volume. The inside had been neatly cut out and the edges of the pages glued together. Within the cavity was a folded square of heavy paper. Gary slowly placed the book on the table and just as slowly removed the paper. He carefully opened it.

"Gary?" said Tuck.

Gary swallowed and then nodded. "Yeh," he said. "May I never speak again if I call you loco, no matter how much I believe it!"

"You're sure that is it?"

Gary spread the chart flat on the table beneath the lamp light. He had seen enough samples of his great-grandfather's handwriting to recognize it instantly on the *derrotero*. In the lower right-hand corner was his great-grandfather's signature. "Yes," he said quietly. "This is it all right, Tuck."

"Let's get out of this creepy place then."

Gary nodded. He folded the *derrotero* and replaced it inside the book, then thrust the book under his arm. He doused the light. Tuck walked past the table, glancing out a window as he did so "Gary!" he said.

"What is it?"

Tuck stepped back from the window. "I'm almost sure I saw someone walking toward the porch."

Gary eased open the library door and moved to the head of the stairs. Tuck came up behind him. It was very quiet—almost too quiet. The faint light of the nearest street lamp came through the painted glass at the top of the front door. The doorknob turned slowly with a little grating noise. The door swung open and the shadowy outline of a man could be seen standing there. He looked toward the stairwell, his face shaded beneath his hat brim. He seemed to be listening. He moved a little and something shone dully in the darkness. A gun or a knife, Gary was sure. The man took a step forward; his hand reached for the stair rail.

Gary took a long chance. "Who is it?" he called out sharply. "Speak up or I start shooting!"

The man spun on a heel and darted awkwardly toward the door. His boots thudded on the porch and then on the stairs. Gary foolishly plunged down the stairs, three at a time. He burst through the doorway and saw a shadowy figure disappear into thick shrubbery at the corner. Gary dashed across the lawn and slipped on slick grass. He came down hard and the book flew from his grasp. Tuck grabbed the book. He looked at the place where the stranger had vanished. "No use chasing him," he said.

Gary disgustedly wiped his muddy hands on the grass. A leaky faucet had allowed a pool to form and the water had soaked into the ground. Gary stood up. The street lamp shone on the wet spot. Boot prints showed clearly, and they were not Gary's prints. Gary bent to look at the strange prints; the left boot print had a clearly marked double crescent of nails and the heel had been nailed crookedly in place. Cold sweat broke out on Gary's face.

"What's wrong?" asked Tuck.

"Let's get out of here!" said Gary. He walked to the house and locked the front door. He ran to the jeep and started the motor. He put the jeep into gear and flicked on the headlights. Something moved quickly in the thick shrubbery at the corner. Gary swung the jeep in as short a turning arc as he could and shifted to second. He was at the corner before he ventured a look back down the shadowy street. There was nothing to be seen. But whoever was hiding in the shrubbery had quite likely seen the book Tuck had picked up.

"Who do you think it was?" asked Tuck.

"It wasn't the Fuller Brush man, *amigo.*"

"No." Tuck peered down the street as Gary turned a corner. "What scared you back there?"

Gary stopped at a stop sign, then drove on again toward the highway. "You remember the boot prints I saw up near that cave?"

"Yes?" Tuck started. He whistled softly. "The same?"

"The same," said Gary.

"Can't this bucket go any faster?"

Gary immediately demonstrated that it could. He wanted to get home and get his hand on his rifle now that they had the *derrotero.* "If you ever find it, keep it to yourself," Jerry Black had advised Gary. "There are men around these mountains who'd do anything to get their hands on it. *Kill even. . . .*"

9 Shadows in the Moonlight

LOBO GREETED THE BOYS at the gate. Gary and Tuck knew then that no one had been prowling about the place. They went into the dark house and pulled the shades in the living room before they put on the lamp. Gary got his Winchester and leaned it against the table. Lobo would warn them if anyone came near the house, giving them time to put out the light.

"This thing gives me the jitters," said Tuck. "Maybe we ought to take someone into our confidence."

"Like who?" snapped Gary. "Jim Kermit? Jerry

Black? Lije Purtis? You loco? We found it and we keep our mouths shut about it."

"All right! All right! It was just a thought," Tuck shrugged. "Still, maybe we ought to hide it for a while before we try to use it. Until things quiet down a little anyways."

"You can't mean that!" said Gary fiercely. "We've been running up blind alleys too long to not use this *derrotero* now that we have it! If you don't come with me tomorrow I'm going it alone!"

"O.K! O.K.! I'm not one to let a buddy go in there alone! Maybe we can be buried together so's our families will only have to put up one tombstone 'stead of two."

"You're a real comedian. Too bad Jerry Lewis isn't looking for a new partner."

"I've got a partner," said Tuck seriously. "Gary, what do you really think about us going into the Espectros?"

Gary sat down and leaned toward his partner. "It isn't as though we were just going in there to take out a couple of burroloads of gold or silver, Tuck. Even with this *derrotero* it isn't going to be easy. Don't forget that the Lost Espectro has been lost for about a hundred years. All my great-grandfather's chart can do for us is to show us what he found, and *he didn't find the lost mine.* Sure, we can follow the clues he has on the *derrotero,* but when we reach the end of them we'll be right where he was when he stopped looking. It's quite possible, too, that someone might have found the Lost Espectro and never opened his mouth."

Don't say such a thing," said Tuck in horror.

"My thought is to leave here before dawn and hike into Cholla Canyon before anyone can see us from higher up, *if* we're being watched. We can take light camping gear along in case we have to stay there overnight."

"Goody, goody," said Tuck. "I can hardly wait."

"Meanwhile let's try to learn this chart by heart. I don't want to take it in there with us."

The two of them sat at the table and studied the *derrotero* with a great deal more interest than they had ever shown in a textbook on algebra or physics. After half an hour Tuck looked up at Gary. "I can compare everything I've seen around the Espectros against this *derrotero* except for one thing, Gary." He placed a finger on a stylized sunburst drawn in a narrow canyon.

"A sunburst like that indicates a mine or mines close by, Tuck. Any symbol of the sun indicates great mineral wealth nearby. The question mark in the center of it was probably my great-grandfather's own idea. Quite likely that sunburst is where he *thought* the mine was."

"That isn't what's bothering me," said Tuck. "Have you ever seen a canyon in those mountains that corresponds to the one he drew and marked with that sunburst?"

Gary shook his head. "That's been bothering me too. I can identify Cholla Canyon and Split Rock Canyon, and the canyon where The Needle is, as well as the canyon where we found the arrastres, but I can't link any canyon in the mountains with that one he has marked."

"Great stuff," said Tuck in disgust. "Then just what good is this *derrotero*?"

"All I know is that he didn't make it to amuse himself. If he marked that canyon on the *derrotero* you can bet your Honda against a dime that *it was there* when he marked it. Jim Kermit's remark that there had been a great many changes in the mountains in the past hundred years sticks in my mind. The day I was working for him I saw up Cholla Canyon to the place where there must have been a landslide years ago. I went the other way and found nothing. I think the place to go is past that landslide."

"Behind The Needle?"

"Yes. A *long* ways behind The Needle. . . ."

Tuck glanced at the clock. "It's getting late. If we're going to do a predawn patrol we'd better get some sleep."

They got their gear ready before they went to bed. Pete Cole's shotgun had been returned and Tuck was to carry it; Gary had his Winchester. "You got any silver bullets, *amigo?*" asked Tuck.

"No, why?"

"Well, I heard lead bullets ain't much good against ghosts but they might work if you rub them with garlic."

"I ought'a rub your pointed little head with garlic!"

"Where do you figure on hiding the *derrotero?*" Gary grinned. "Atop the windmill platform," he said. "No one would think of looking for it there."

"No one but an eagle, that is."

It was pitch dark outside. Gary crossed swiftly to the windmill and quietly scaled the ladder. He secreted the *derrotero* beneath a loose board. He did not return to the ground immediately. He felt as though he was atop the mast of a sailing ship far out on the dark sea. The Espectros were dark and hulking against the night sky; the lights of The Wells could be seen in the clear air. There was a breathless feeling within Gary. Tomorrow might reveal the long-lost secret of the treasure of the Espectros.

A cold dawn wind swept along the lower reaches of Cholla Canyon as Gary led the way through the tangled brush to where he had found the first symbol. It was still very dark in the big canyon, and even Lobo was subdued, trailing closely at Gary's heels, with Tuck not far behind. Several times during the night the big dog had barked, awakening the boys, but nothing had happened. They had not shown a light at the house when they had arisen, breakfasted, and left the premises in the thick darkness of the hour before dawn.

It was hard going until the first faint light of the false dawn began to show in the sky. By that time the boys had reached the place where the branch canyon split off to the right hand. Gary looked up the dark slopes toward the unseen cave. It was as quiet as the grave. He shuddered at the simile.

Gary swiftly crossed the mouth of the branch canyon and began to fight his way through the vicious tangle that almost filled the narrow upper end of Cholla Canyon. It was quite obvious that there had been a vast slide of earth and rocks in years past. It was also obvious that the rushing waters of many flash floods had gouged the narrow passage to one side of the slide. The dawn light was filtering down into the canyon. High above them were masses of dry brush wedged into crevices; here and there bleached pieces of driftwood hung like bones of the long dead. They were the markers indicating the height of the floods that poured through that canyon. It wasn't a pleasant sight. The Espectros seemed to breed vicious storms in the late summer and early fall, and to be caught in a canyon at such a time was akin to a death sentence.

Beyond the slide it was possible to see no more than a few hundred yards at a time because of the devious and tortured way of the deep canyon. Despite the coolness of the early morning the boys were running with sweat as they forced their way through clinging catclaw and savage jumping cholla that seemed to snap at them in anger. They rounded a right-hand bend. Gary stopped and eyed a huge overhanging cliff, shaped like the cup of a gigantic clamshell. "The *derrotero* shows water in here, Tuck," he said over his shoulder.

Tuck wiped the sweat from his face. "What's that up there?" He pointed to the cliff face. Clearly marked was a Spanish gourd, the unmistakable symbol for water in the vicinity.

It was Lobo who found the spring. It welled up

from beneath a rock face to form a shallow pool in a *hueco* or rock hollow. The three of them drank the cold, sweet water. Tuck wiped his mouth and reached for his haversack. "Time for lunch?"

"It's hardly nine o'clock," said Gary. "I'll go ahead and see what's up there."

"Watch yourself, *amigo.*"

"I wasn't thinking of getting careless."

Gary was a good five hundred yards east of the spring when he found the narrow slit that marked a branch canyon trending off to the right, deep in shadow, cold, and forbidding. He turned to look up the main canyon and saw a chiseled outline on a great slab of fallen rock. It was the outline of a tortoise. There was no way of telling to which of the two canyons it had originally pointed.

Tuck floundered through the brush and eyed the rock. "Got a little lonely back there," he said. "What's that?"

"The tortoise symbol has various meanings. Sometimes the head points toward treasure, or buried possessions nearby."

"Go on."

Gary looked at his friend. "It can also mean death, defeat, or destruction . . ."

"But that was years ago, wasn't it?" asked Tuck in a very small voice.

"It has to be one way or the other." Gary took a coin from his pocket and flipped it high into the air. "Heads to the left. Tails to the right." He caught it deftly. "Tails," he said quietly.

Tuck eyed the narrow, uninviting passageway. "Best out of three?" he suggested weakly.

Gary shook his head. There was really no choice. If they went up the main canyon and could not find any further symbols they would have to explore the narrower canyon anyway. He led the way. Their footsteps echoed hollowly as though they had entered a vast and empty vault carved into the very heart of the Espectros. Neither of them spoke. Silence seemed to be the ground rule in that dark and echoing place. Silence, and a constant feeling of something watching and waiting for anyone fool enough to look for the Lost Espectro.

The heat of the midmorning sun had begun to penetrate into the canyons by the time the two explorers came to a widening of the canyon they were in. "Just where are we?" asked Tuck.

"We're heading southerly. I think we're roughly parallel to The Needle Canyon, but I haven't any idea how far we are from it."

"You think this canyon comes out on the south side of the Espectros?"

"If it doesn't we'll either have to backtrack or stay in here tonight."

So far they had seen no guiding symbols. That is, until Tuck fell over a rock. Gary gave him a hand to help him to his feet, and as he did so he saw something through a screen of brush. It was another gourd symbol pointing back to the way they had come. That wasn't much help, but at least it indicated that the Mexican miners had been in there.

Tuck picked a cactus needle from his hand and looked ahead. He silently pointed at something. On an overhanging rock had been chiseled a deep Roman cross. "That's another marking with a number of meanings," said Gary. "It might mean there are church treasures buried in here, which isn't likely. It also means a Christian has passed this way. If it was lying on its side instead of being upright, then the long part of the cross would point to the treasure trail."

"As far as we're concerned then, that marking doesn't mean much."

Gary looked up at the high rims of the canyon. "It was cut in here for a reason, maybe as protection against something evil."

They moved on slowly, scanning the canyon walls for more markings. An hour passed before they found another symbol and again it was the gourd marking, still pointing in the direction from which they had come. A sluggish wind stirred in the canyon but it brought little relief from the gathering heat of the day. The canyon began to angle to the right with a rather sharp turn visible in the distance. The canyon floor became a mass of tumbled and riven rock intermingled and laced together by thorny brush and scrubby trees. Here and there shattered tree trunks showed in the jumble.

"I sure could use a drink," said Tuck as he wiped his face.

Lobo moved ahead of them, to vanish in the tangle. In a few minutes he returned and his black muzzle was wet with water. Gary forced his way through a last screen of brush and stopped in astonishment. Before him was a wide shallow pool that had formed in the lowest part of the canyon floor. Scum floated on the surface of the water at his feet, but it seemed clearer at the base of the eastern wall of the canyon. He walked to the wall and tasted the clear water. It was fresh and sweet and it seemed to well from the naked rock itself.

Tuck dropped on his belly and drank deeply. "Sure needed that," he said. "Let's eat." He eyed Gary. "What's the matter?"

Gary looked up and down the heat-soaked canyon. "Strange," he said quietly. "The gourd symbols point the other way."

"So?"

"If there was water here, why would they show signs to the spring so far behind us? Besides, from what I remember from the *derrotero,* there wasn't any symbol on that either indicating the presence of a spring in *here.*"

Tuck was gnawing at a sandwich. He eyed the pool. "Seems to come from under that wall," he said.

Gary looked up. There was no symbol for a spring marked on that sheer face of rock.

They ate and then filled their canteens. As much as Gary wanted to continue the search, he knew it was only a matter of a few hours before the canyon would be dark in shadows. A quarter of a mile beyond the water hole they found another symbol carved into a pinnacle of rock that jutted out from the right-hand wall of the canyon. It was a neatly depicted outline of a bowie knife, pointing back in the direction from which they had come. "Trail to mine or treasure; travel on," translated Gary.

"Maybe it means travel on to the next gourd symbol," suggested Tuck.

"No. The meaning is clear enough." Gary pushed on ahead and was rewarded fifteen minutes later by finding the next symbol, a mule shoe lying horizontally. "En route to treasure; keep traveling," said Gary. He turned and looked down the shadowed canyon. "It must be *behind* us," he said. "The symbols for water pointed the other way, away from the spring we found. Now the symbols here do not indicate that there is water just ahead, but rather to treasure. Also behind us . . ."

Tuck shoved back his hat. "And the symbols in Cholla Canyon indicated that we come *this* way. I agree. The treasure, if there is any, has to be behind us, and between the last water symbol and that bowie knife symbol back there. Maybe the cross symbol indicated that the treasure was *there*."

Gary shook his head. "I don't think so."

"Maybe we ought to try the *horqueta*?" Tuck rummaged in his bulging haversack and came up with a Y-shaped bone, the bleached scapula of some long-dead animal. He inverted the bone so that the leg of the Y was upward, and tapped a glass knob which had been set into the tip of the bone. There was a threaded hole drilled in the glass knob. Tuck fumbled in the haversack again.

"You think the Lost Espectro was a gold or silver mine?"

"Gold," said Gary.

Tuck selected a screw from the number he had taken from the haversack. He screwed it into the hole in the glass knob. "Let's go," he said cheerfully. He gripped the two lower prongs of bone in his hands, thumbs out and palms upward.

"*What* is *that?*"

Tuck grinned. "Ol' Emilio Chavez traded me this for a double-barreled shotgun. You hold it like I'm holding it, then wait to feel the 'pull' of the minerals. That screw happens to have a speck of gold dust in it. Now if it were silver we were looking for, or copper, or whatever, we'd put in the screw with *that* mineral, you see. The screws are hollow and filled with a bit of the mineral you are hunting. Like attracts like, *amigo*. Emilio said it was infallible. Always works. Now . . ." His voice died away as he saw the look on Gary's face.

"If everything Emilio cons you into taking is infallible, how come Emilio Chavez is the poorest man in The Wells?"

"Well, now that you mention it," said Tuck thoughtfully.

"Tuckie," said Gary in his kindliest tone, "put one of those screws in the hollow place in your head. It's the sun, I think, or maybe your mother dropped you on your soft little head when you were a baby."

While they stood there the sun suddenly vanished and thicker shadows filled the canyon. A cool wind began to feel its way through the darkness.

"We'll keep moving on," said Gary. "We can make better time when the moon comes up. O.K.? Or would you rather camp in here tonight?"

Tuck smiled wanly as he stored his precious *horqueta* away.

The darkness grew and thickened. The boys did not speak to each other. There was something in the atmosphere of that forbidding place that banned conversation. Now and then they stopped their slow progress to listen. They saw the velvety-winged flight of the night-hunting owl and heard the pitiful squeaking of a mouse caught in the steely talons of that same owl. They heard the swift and almost noiseless passages of nocturnal animals through the brush. The dry wind crept through the canyon, moaning softly through crevices.

It seemed like an eternity before the first faint suggestion of moonrise appeared in the sky. Then gradually, almost imperceptibly, they could distinguish objects and see the path beneath their tired and aching feet. The lighter it grew, the faster they traveled, and in so doing, they became careless about noise. If someone or *something* was listening to their passage . . .

They reached a place where the canyon widened. Lobo stopped trotting at Gary's heels. A low growl sounded deep in his throat. He laid back his stub ears and his hackles arose. Gary moved toward the canyon wall and knelt beside the big dog. "Quiet, Lobo," he whispered. "Quiet now!"

The three of them watched and waited. The canyon floor was silvered with cold moonlight, etching sharply each shadow. Nothing moved except the wind. Minutes ticked past, and then Gary felt the hard muscles of the dog tighten against his arm. Tuck wet his lips. He pointed out toward the center of the canyon. The shadows were still motionless, and then one of them seemed to move. But there was nothing there to give body to that shadow. It seemed to move steadily and independently, drifting across rocks and brush. The shadow stopped, then moved on again. Gary saw now that it was the shadow of a hatless man. *But there was no man to form that shadow!*

Tuck touched Gary on the shoulder and jerked

a thumb upward. Gary understood now. Whoever it was, standing on the rim of the canyon, high overhead; the moonlight came from behind him, throwing his bodiless shadow onto the canyon floor. The shadow moved. It bent its head as though to listen. Something pattered dryly on the ground just to the right of the boys. It must be something living up there—rather than a ghost—to be able to push gravel over the edge of the rim.

Cold fear raced through Gary. His legs and stomach seemed to get weak. He swallowed hard, almost afraid to breathe for fear of making a sound. The gravel pattered closer. Tuck's breathing became louder and more irregular. Gary felt as though he were held in subjection to the thing up there. It was quite enough fear for him that night. There was a limit.

Gary jumped to his feet and grabbed his rifle. He ran swiftly out into the center of the canyon. He turned and clearly saw a hatless man standing at the edge of the rim looking down at him, but Gary could not see the shadowed face. "Who are you? What do you want?" he demanded angrily.

The man raised a rifle. Gary threw up his own gun and fired high over the unknown's head. He slammed out three more rapid-fire rounds. The man jumped out of sight. The crashing echoes bounded and rebounded between the canyon walls in roaring confusion.

"You loco?" screamed Tuck.

Gary waved Tuck on. Lobo sped toward Gary, barking deeply. Gary wasted no time. Tired as he was his feet fairly seemed to fly over the rough ground. This time Tuck did not pass him. They were half a mile down the canyon when Gary threw himself on the ground to regain his breath. Tuck staggered up and fell down beside him. There was now no sign of life up the moonlit canyon.

When they had their breath back they trudged on to the south. Far ahead of them they could see where the canyon floor slanted down toward the distant desert, silvered by the moonlight.

The haunting cry arose behind them like the dire wailing of a doomed soul, echoing eerily down the canyon until at last it died away. This time the boys did not stop for breath nor look back until they reached the hidden mouth of the canyon.

10 Clues from the Sky

THE MOON HAD DIED, leaving behind it an intense darkness that cloaked the mountains with only the wolf-fanged peaks showing against the dark blue blanket of the sky. Two tired boys trudged toward the Cole ranch house. Gary turned to look at Tuck. "We still have two days," he said, "in which to hunt." He eyed his lean companion. Tuck had hardly spoken since they had emerged from the mouth of the canyon into the desert. Maybe Tucker C. Browne had his belly full of treasure hunting.

Tuck yawned. He trudged on, shifting his shotgun from one shoulder to the other.

"Tuck?" said Gary uneasily. He himself wanted to keep on searching, but he'd hardly want to do it without Tuck.

Tuck yawned again. "Well, kid, it's like this," he said quietly. He paused.

"Go on, Tuck! Say it! You want to quit!"

Tuck turned slowly. "What's with you?" he said in astonishment. "I was about to say we've got as good a lead as we could wish. It's a lead-pipe cinch that the treasure *has* to be back there beyond that water hole. I figure we can go right back into the canyon we just left. One of us can stand guard while the other hunts for more symbols."

"What about that man, or *thing*, we saw back there?"

Tuck spat indelicately. "Well, if it was a ghost, he won't be around during daylight hours. If it was a man, he knows we mean business. Man, you scared the Hades out of me when you opened up on him." Tuck grinned. "If that wasn't a ghost, I'll just bet whoever it was, was a mite worried himself with all that lead whistling over his head. Hawww!"

Gary couldn't help but grin himself. Then he

looked down at Lobo. The dog had hunched his shoulders and was standing still, looking intently toward the darkened house. "Wait," said Gary quickly to Tuck.

They stood there in the windy darkness. The windmill creaked softly. There was no other sound. "Go on, Lobo," said Gary. He loaded his rifle. The dog trotted ahead and squirmed beneath a wire fence. The two boys climbed over it and eyed the house. The dog padded on, circled the house, then came back. He looked up at Gary as though to let him know it was all right to go to the house.

Gary opened the back door and walked in. Until he lighted the room there was a tautness of fear within him. He stared at the once immaculate kitchen. It was a shambles. Drawers hung open, tea towels were scattered on the floor, cabinet doors gaped and even the oven door hung open. Tuck whistled softly. "Mice?" he suggested.

Lobo padded into the living room, followed by the boys. The room was a mess. Chair cushions had been removed, table drawers opened, books tumbled from the shelves, the rug peeled back, and the couch overturned, with the padding slit open by a knife.

It was Gary's room that had suffered the most damage. The mattress had been torn to pieces.

The lining had been pulled loose from the closet. His books were scattered all over. The pockets of his clothing had been pulled out. Gary felt sick. He looked at Tuck. "Oh, Lord," he said, "you were supposed to be watching the place until I got back."

"Yeh," said Tuck with a weak grin. He looked about. "I don't think we have any doubt about what they were looking for in here."

Gary shook his head. "The windmill," he said quickly. "I wonder?"

"Don't go near it now!" warned Tuck.

"There'd be no one watching nearby," said Gary. "Lobo would let us know."

Tuck shrugged. "Shall we risk it?"

Gary walked to the front door. He flicked off the lights and peered through the glass window set in the door. It was as dark as the inside of a boot out there—a mysterious, clinging darkness that seemed to be a menace in itself. He eased open the door. "Take a look, Lobo," he said in a low voice.

The dog vanished in the darkness. In a few minutes he was back and he dropped to his belly on the porch. Gary walked to the windmill and looked up the ladder. It was possible that a person at a distance might be able to skyline him up there. It wasn't a pleasant thought, and a .50/110 slug could bore a big hole in a man. He climbed slowly and as quietly as possible, reached the top, felt beneath the loose board, and almost panicked. The *derrotero* was not there!

He clung to the ladder and peered out into the darkness, wondering who or what was out there. Perhaps the person who had removed the *derrotero* was still somewhere nearby. There was a green sickness within him. To find the *derrotero* after years of search and then to lose it again! He eased his hand beneath the board and felt along it. Something rustled dryly and fell from the platform. He almost panicked again. Swiftly he descended the ladder and dropped to hands and kness, pawing the damp ground. When at last his hands closed on the folded chart, he breathed a silent prayer, then hurried back to the house. He did not feel at ease until the door had been locked and barred behind him. He wordlessly handed the *derrotero* to Tuck, who took it as though it were red hot. He juggled it a little. "What do *I* do with it?" he asked.

Gary leaned against the wall. "We'd better take it with us tomorrow. Right now I'm going to get some sleep. I want to be out of here before dawn, as we were this morning."

Tuck nodded. "I'll take the first watch," he said. "Tired as I am, I can't sleep right now."

Gary walked into his room and lifted the ripped mattress onto his bed. It was no time to be choosy. He pulled off his hat and boots and dropped onto the mattress. It seemed as though he were asleep the instant he hit it.

When he opened his eyes again it was still dark. He had no idea as to what time it was. The house was deathly quiet. He sat up and dropped his legs over the side of the bed. Something seemed to warn him as he sat there; he reached for his rifle and then stood up. He stood there for a few minutes, listening with cocked head for a sound. Gary walked softly to the bedroom door and through the dark hallway to the living room. Gentle and steady breathing sounded from the couch. Gary tiptoed across the littered room and looked down at Tuck, sound asleep, faithful as ever to his trust. He couldn't help but grin. He was a little startled when the pendulum clock struck one. It seemed much later than that. He reached out to arouse Tuck and his hand stopped midway. A grating noise came from the back of the house.

Gary turned quickly. Lobo was either sound asleep or had wandered off, as he often did at odd hours. The kitchen door squeaked as it was opened, and Gary remembered then that he had not locked it. He reached down and clamped a hand on Tuck's mouth. He looked down into Tuck's wide eyes and shook his head, then released his grasp. Tuck stood up and reached for his shotgun but Gary again shook his head. The scatter-gun was too dangerous in close quarters.

Something moved just beyond the doorway to the kitchen. Gary pointed down, tapped his chest, pointed up, and touched Tuck's chest. His sign language was clear. They'd take the intruder by force, Gary in low and Tuck on high. Somebody loomed in the doorway and Gary drove in hard, arms outspread to grip the legs while Tuck closed in. The stranger thrust out a balled fist and Tuck smacked into it and grunted in pain as he fell sideways to land on top of Gary. The intruder broke loose. Tuck came up and caught a boot heel against his chin. Down he went again. Gary darted after the intruder as he ran for the back door and dived for him, catching him about the waist and driving him hard against the wall. Fingernails clawed Gary's face. "Let me go, you big ape!" screamed a thoroughly feminine voice.

"It's Sue!" yelled Tuck. "We might have known she'd be nosing around."

Gary could feel the blood running down his face. She had put up one whale of a defense. "Don't put on a light," he warned Tuck. He pulled the blinds on the windows and locked the door.

"Man," said Tuck. "I ran right into that fist of yours, Susie. Were you holding a flatiron in it?"

She laughed shakily. "I was so scared I didn't know what I was doing."

"I'd hate to see you in action when you *did* know what you were doing," said Gary ruefully.

"I didn't want to disturb anyone," she said. "Besides, I wasn't sure you were here. Lobo wasn't around."

"He usually isn't when we need him," said Tuck.

"Would you mind telling us how you happened to come here at this hour?" asked Gary.

"Well, I was going to stay with Francie Kermit this weekend," she said.

"Just by coincidence," said Tuck dryly. "I never thought you and Francie were buddy-buddy. The only reason you were going to stay there was to keep an eye on us."

"What difference does it make?" she said. "Don't answer that! Well anyway, Mr. Kermit is gone for the weekend."

Gary looked quickly at Tuck. "I wonder?" he

said, thinking of the shadowy figure that had been watching them.

"Wonder what?" asked Sue.

"Nothing," said Tuck. "Go on with your lying, Cousin Sue."

"Well, Mr. Kermit had left something for Gary at the house. I wanted to bring it right over, but Francie said it could wait until tomorrow, *today* I mean. I couldn't sleep. So I sneaked out of the house and came over here."

"You could have got killed," said Tuck fiercely.

They could see her inspecting her nails. "Oh, I don't know," she said archly.

"Listen to her!" snapped Tuck.

"Forget it," said Gary. "What was it he left for me?"

She took out a roll of heavy paper from within her shirt and handed it to Gary. He got a bull's-eye lantern from a cabinet and lighted it, holding it close to the floor so that no glow would show through the blinds. It cast a bright circle of light on the floor. Gary unrolled the paper and saw that it was an aerial photograph—an aerial photograph of mountains cut with deep twisting canyons. His breath caught in his throat. "The Espectros!" he said excitedly. He looked up at her. "Tell me about this!"

"He wasn't there when I got there. Francie said that he told her he found out that one copy of the aerial photograph made during the war was still in the files of *The Cottonwood Wells Courier,* so he picked it up for you."

Gary eyed the photograph. "The negatives were destroyed in a fire at the airfield and Jim told me he didn't know who had any prints of them."

"That was darned nice of him," said Tuck.

"I wonder?" said Gary quietly.

"What do you mean?" asked Tuck.

Gary stood up and turned off the lantern. "Maybe Jim Kermit has been looking for the Lost Espectro all these years without any luck. Perhaps Jim figured that we might find it with the help of this photograph coupled with what we already know. He'd let us go poking into those canyons, trailing us maybe, until we did find the mine, then close in for the kill."

"How you talk!" said Sue. "After he was nice enough to get that photograph for you!" Her voice changed. "Is he a prime suspect, Gary?"

"Forget that TV talk," said Tuck. He paced back and forth. "He's not at home this weekend. Who knows where he really is? Might be outside right now. Maybe he was at your grandfather's house in The Wells when we found the *derrotero* there . . ." His voice trailed off. His eyes widened. He clamped a hand over his mouth.

Sue seemed to expand a little in the darkness. "So," she said slowly, "you *did* find the *derrotero*?"

"You and your big flapping mouth!" moaned Gary to Tuck. "Well, she knows now!" He picked up the photograph and the lantern and took them to the little windowless room next to his where he kept his relics and other odds and ends. He put the photograph on the table, then placed the faded and wrinkled *derrotero* beside it. He did not look up as the other two quietly entered the room behind him. Gary traced a finger up Cholla Canyon on the photograph and located the water hole, hardly more than a dot on the narrow floor of the long canyon. To the east of the canyon and slightly north, the terrain seemed a lighter hue, hardly distinguishable from the rest of the land, but still obviously lighter. He studied the *derrotero*. The sunburst with the question mark in it was marked to the east of the water-hole canyon in yet another canyon, nothing more than a narrow slot in the rough terrain, but plainly marked on the *derrotero*. *There was no such canyon apparent on the photograph.*

Tuck traced the line of another twisting, narrow canyon. "That's where we found the arrastres," he said. He moved his finger to the right and placed it on the area where the canyon showed on the *derrotero* but not on the photograph. "It figures," he added. "There was a canyon there in the old days, in the time of your great-grandfather, Gary, that could be reached both from Cholla Canyon and the canyon of the arrastres. It isn't there now, that's for sure."

"Buried forever in a landslide," said Gary gloomily. He reached for a magnifying glass he used on his rock specimens and began to study the photograph inch by inch. The lighter area held his attention. There wasn't any doubt in his mind that the lighter area indicated the massive slide. He noted, too, that on the *derrotero* water was indicated as flowing down the canyon of the arrastres, but no water showed on the photograph. He looked for the time of the year when the photograph had been made. It had been taken in the wintertime and there surely should have been drainage water in the canyon at that time. Yet no water showed there. But water did show in the photograph of the narrow canyon they had explored, and *did not show on the derrotero.* Surely his great-grandfather would have marked such an important thing as a water hole in that dry land. Then, too, the very carved symbols in the canyon did not indicate water there, but rather farther on, at the spring they had found in the upper reaches of Cholla Canyon. So there had been no water in there during the time of the Mexican miners either. "No wonder the Lost Espectro has never been found," he said. "The land changes have been too great." He quickly related his thoughts to his two friends.

Tuck placed a finger on the water hole they had found. "The key is right here somewhere," he said. "You think it's possible that the landslide may have diverted the original water source in the canyon of the arrastres back into the canyon where we found the water hole?"

"I'm almost sure of it," said Gary. He passed a hand over the lighter area of the terrain. "I wonder how many thousands and thousands of tons of rock may be atop the Lost Espectro?"

"It won't hurt to look," said Sue courageously.

"Who said anything about *you* going?" demanded Tuck.

Again the fingernails were inspected. "When I tell the story about how two rough, tough juniors from Cottonwood Wells Union High School tangled with a little slip of a girl and darned near got whipped this summer, I wonder how your standing will be?"

"You wouldn't!" said Tuck.

"Just you try me, Mister Tucker C. Browne!"

"She would too," said Tuck to Gary.

A cold anger grew within Gary. "All right," he said harshly. "I'm sick of her poking her nose into everything we do. If she wants to risk it, I don't care! We're going back into that canyon today."

"When?" asked Tuck.

"I'm not sleepy. How can you sleep at a time like this?"

"Who said anything about sleeping? I was hoping you'd want to go right now."

Gary rolled the *derrotero* and the photograph together and wrapped them in plastic sheeting. "I don't want to stay around here any longer than I have to."

Sue grinned and the lantern light glistened on her braces.

"No wonder, the way you characters have been keeping house. What a mess!"

Tuck raised his eyes toward the ceiling. "Lord," he breathed, "make me strong. We didn't mess up the house, Sue! It was that way when we got back. Somebody must have been searching for the *derrotero*."

"Oh," she said in a small, weak voice.

"Now do you want to stay behind?" asked Tuck.

"No," she said firmly.

"Well," he said in resignation, "I have only one deep consolation. Being a female, you'll probably get married some day to some unfortunate male, which means you have to change your name from Browne to whatever *his* name is, which makes me, as your beloved first cousin, happy indeed!"

"Enough of that," said Gary. "This is no class picnic we're going on. It might be dangerous in there. It's bad enough that Tuck and I are taking this chance, Sue, without involving you too. You've been a big help and we appreciate it, but you're going to have to take orders from us. Is that clear?"

"I like taking orders from you, Gary," she said.

Tuck grunted and rolled his eyes up. "We have to have *one* leader. I nominate Gary Cole. Any seconds?"

"I second the nomination," said Sue.

"Motion made and seconded. Any objections? None? Those in favor say aye. Aye!"

"Aye!" said Sue.

"Motion made and carried. All hail, Leader!"

"That means you have to take orders from me too," said Gary with a grin.

Tuck frowned. "I never thought of it that way."

"Let's get moving. We'll need our gear, digging tools, rope, food, guns, and one blanket apiece."

"Why?" asked Sue.

"We might have to stay in there overnight."

She smiled weakly. "Oh," she said.

"We'll take the jeep toward the highway, then cut east on the old gravel road," said Gary. "We can leave the jeep about a mile from the canyon mouth and walk in. It will still be dark. We can make the water hole about dawn. You still sure you want to come along, Sue?"

"Absolutely."

"On your head be it," said Tuck.

They wasted no time thereafter. While they were loading the jeep, Lobo, as though conjured up by magic, appeared in the dimness and jumped casually into the back seat. Gary started the jeep and drove out to the road, turned left, and headed for the highway. Before he reached the main highway he shut off the headlights, then turned left onto the old gravel road. They wouldn't be fooling anyone who might have watched them leave the house, but the desert was wide and dark, so the chance was worth taking that they might get away with it. Gary really didn't care as much as he thought he would. He was sure they were on the right trail this time. The next day or two would decide if the mine was buried forever, or if the Lost Espectro really could be found.

11 Into the Heart of the Espectros

THE WATER HOLE was a sheet of smooth pewter-colored liquid in the faint cold light of dawn.

Something splashed in the water and then came the scurrying of small feet on the hard ground and a rustling in the brush as some small animal fled from the pool. The concentric ripples spread smoothly and began to lap softly on the shore. The faint musical sound died away and the canyon was as quiet as before.

Tuck took up position as guard in the thick tangle where he could see both rims of the canyon. Gary placed Sue near the water hole and told Lobo to stay with her. Gary pushed on, scanning the wall of the eastern side. There was nothing to be seen. Two hundred yards beyond the water hole he came to a huge, tiptilted slab of rock which forced him to step down into a deep hollow. He was about to pass on when he saw the carving beneath the slab. He crouched to see it clearly. It was the familiar equilateral triangle with the curved line sprouting from the tip, pointing onward, indicating the treasure trail was around a bend or curve.

Gary stepped up out of the hole. The huge slab had obviously been moved by great brute force from its original position to lie so. He walked up the canyon in the pale watery light. Beyond him there was no indication of a curve or bend to the right, as the symbol indicated, nor was there even a bend or curve to the left. The canyon here was as straight as a mine drift. It was then that he noticed the formation of the canyon wall. It was made up of tumbled and shattered rock, bleached wood, and tangled brush. He compared it to the rock of the west wall, which was darker and smooth, almost as though it had been polished. It was quite evident then that the bend or curve indicated by the symbol no longer existed; it had been filled in by huge masses of fallen rock and earth.

He scanned the walls, both old and new, and saw no symbols. He turned and trudged back toward the water hole. He squatted at the edge of it and looked at the slightly disturbed surface of the water right where the rock wall met it. "Go get Tuck," he said to Sue. "You take guard. Don't do anything if you see anything suspicious. Let us know."

She hurried off. Tuck scrambled through the brush and squatted beside Gary. "Speak, O Leader," he said.

Gary told him of his deduction. Tuck nodded wisely. Gary dabbled a hand in the cool water. "You said it might have been possible for the land changes to have forced the water that used to run down the canyon of the arrastres into this canyon, Tuck," he said quietly. "Supposing we could trace the source of this water? Maybe it might lead us to the Lost Espectros."

"That's loco," said Tuck. He looked up at the towering canyon wall above them. "We can't get over that."

"Maybe we can go *under* it," said Gary. He stood up and peeled off his shirt. "I'm going for a swim."

Tuck watched him with wide eyes as he stripped to his shorts and waded into the pool. Gary walked to the wall and began to feel along it under the surface of the water. His hands probed into nothingness. He took several deep breaths, held the last one, and submerged, leaving a series of ripples that lapped at Tuck's feet. Tuck Browne closed his eyes and prayed for the first time in a long while.

Gary rose a little and his head struck solid rock. He dived down again, felt his knees scrape the rough gravel bottom, and then came cautiously upward again. When his head broke the water, he found himself in a domed cavern illuminated from some dim source ahead of him. He swam slowly to the side of the cavern and crawled out onto a narrow ledge, shivering from mingled cold and fear. He realized now that his swim had been a very short one. He could hardly be more than twenty feet from where he had started. It had seemed such a long one, but all out of proportion as when one's tongue explores a tooth cavity and magnifies it tremendously.

Gary stood up and began to explore the ledge. There was shattered driftwood scattered along it. A cheerful thought, for the water had brought it into the cavern from outside. But how *far* outside? He walked forward slowly and saw that the ledge petered out. He took a staff of driftwood and probed the dark water; it was about two feet deep. He waded in and followed a bend in the cavern, testing the depth all the way. Then suddenly everything seemed clear to the eye and he waded out into a narrow slot of a canyon, if one could correctly call it that, hardly more than twenty feet wide. High, high above him was the sky, now lighted with the rising of the sun. To his right was a narrow strand, littered with dead brush and driftwood. He waded to it and walked along it. He could see fairly far ahead. Gary shivered. The deep, narrow trough seemed to penetrate into the very bowels of the Espectros.

He returned to the cavern and eyed the dark and uninviting surface of the water, dreading the thought of having to enter it again. Something scuttled over his bare feet and he almost screamed in sudden panic. He saw that it was a gecko lizard scuttling toward the dark wall at the forward end of the cavern. Lizards were usually creatures of the sunlight. He walked to the place where he had seen the lizard vanish and got down on his hands and knees. He was relieved to see a faint line of light. He got down on his belly and squirmed beneath the rock. There was soft earth beneath him. He shoved some of it aside and crawled out into broad daylight to look up into the grinning face of Tucker C. Browne. "Dr. Livingstone, I presume," said that worthy.

Gary dressed quickly. Tuck got Sue. The two of them listened to Gary's story. "So," concluded Gary, "the only clue left to the lost mine, at least in my opinion, is the canyon beyond the cavern."

There was a long and deathly silence from the two Brownes.

"I'm going back in," said Gary quietly.

"I'll side you," said Tuck.

"Me too," said Sue.

"No," said Tuck.

"You can't leave me here," said Sue stubbornly.

She was right. While Gary widened the entrance to the cavern, Tuck and Sue got the gear. Gary carried it into the cavern. The two Brownes came in, followed by Lobo. The dog trotted ahead along the narrow ledge. "Aladdin's Cave," said Sue. "Who's got the magic lantern?"

Lobo turned suddenly. He trotted back past the three of them and began to growl. Gary stared at him. Suddenly there was darkness beneath the wall as rock and dirt fell heavily. Gary ran forward and got down on his knees. The hole had been blocked. He pushed against the rocks and could not move them. A cold feeling of dread came over him.

"Rock fall?" said Tuck from behind Gary.

'Maybe," said Gary. He stood up and looked at his two companions.

"We can always swim under the wall," said Sue.

"You might as well face the truth," said Gary. "If that wasn't a rock fall, someone blocked that hole, and that same someone could be waiting for us to pop up out of the water."

"Like who?" asked Tuck.

"Whom!" corrected Sue.

Gary shrugged. "Someone might have been watching us all the time," he said.

"Well, if we can't get out, he can't get in," said Sue.

"Yeh," said Tuck. He shivered.

Another cold thought came to Gary. They were unable to return through the hole, but that did not mean whoever had blocked the hole could not clear it and follow them if he so desired.

Gary took his gear and waded into the water. He led the way out into the tunnel-like canyon. There was no way to scale those sheer walls. He walked on, keeping his face turned away from the others so that they might not see the fear etched upon it.

They splashed steadily onward, sometimes wading, sometimes clambering over loose detritus that had fallen from high above. The echoes of their slow passage made strange and eerie sounds as though someone, or *something,* was laughing at them.

Now and again they had to squeeze between the damp walls which had closed in together. If a flash flood should strike suddenly, as they often did, it would fill the narrow trough with roaring waters that would drown anything living caught in the canyon.

After an hour's slow progress they stopped to rest. Gary unwrapped the *derrotero* and the photograph to study them. He took out his compass and checked the direction in which they were traveling. It was almost due east. Yet the canyon they were in did not show on the *derrotero* or on the aerial photograph. The three of them discussed it quietly. "It's possible that the photograph might not have picked up this canyon. Sometimes at certain angles, things can be hidden," said Tuck.

Gary took out his magnifying glass and studied the photograph of the general area in which they now were. Suddenly he started. His lens had caught a very faint line, barely discernible, running along the mesa top in an easterly direction from the canyon of the water hole. He eyed it closely but he could not distinguish any features.

"This might be the canyon we are in," he said, tracing the line with his finger. "Maybe you're right, Tuck. The light or angle—or something—might not have caught the canyon quite right."

"But it's not marked on the *derrotero*," said Sue.

"Which means it either did not exist at the time the *derrotero* was made, or my great-grandfather left it out because it had no bearing on the treasure trail," said Gary. He tapped the sunburst marking with the question mark inside of the circle. "But from what I can figure, this *has* to be ahead of us. With luck, this canyon might just run into the canyon where the sunburst has been marked on the *derrotero*."

"And if it doesn't?" asked Sue.

Gary did not answer. He rolled photograph and *derrotero* together and replaced them in the plastic wrapping.

"Maybe this canyon doesn't lead anywhere," said Sue. "Maybe it is a dead end. What do we do then, partners?"

"Go back," said Gary shortly.

Her eyes were wide and her face was taut. "But what if . . . ? Say he is . . . ?"

Gary walked on, followed by Tuck. Both of them were just as concerned as Sue was, but the lure of the Lost Espectro took precedence over their concern and fright.

The morning was at mid-passage when they reached a place where the canyon widened. The right-hand side of the canyon was still that sheer wall, so steep and high it seemed to be leaning over the canyon, but the left-hand side was now lower and composed of shattered rock and great boulders stippled with long-dead trees and brush, a treacherous-looking and impassable mass. Here the canyon trended to the left and narrowed again, and on the left-hand side appeared a dark opening from which the stream emerged, much as it had back in the canyon of the water hole.

Tuck eyed the dark orifice and shivered a little. "We have to go in there now?" he said.

Gary grounded his rifle and looked farther up the narrowing canyon. "Not until we see what is up there. This is evidently the place where the stream broke through when it was blocked from the canyon of the arrastres. *¡Adelante!*" He led the way to the east.

The sun was at its zenith when they reached a place where their narrow passageway joined yet another canyon, and despite the light of the sun, this was a gloomy place, for the walls leaned inward, forming a rough bottle shape, with the mouth of the great bottle high overhead. There was a strange brooding quality about this place that repelled Gary. Lobo growled low in his throat and pressed his muscular body hard against Gary's leg.

"I'd almost rather go into that water cave back there," said Tuck. "This place is downright creepy."

Once again Gary checked *derrotero* and aerial photograph against each other. This time he was quite sure that the sunburst with the question mark inscribed inside of it must be quite close, but there was no indication on the aerial photograph that such a canyon as the one that loomed before them existed at all. If the sunburst *was* in that canyon, it was an indication that his great-grandfather had in all likelihood penetrated in there, but the question mark within the circle of the sunburst clearly indicated that either he had not believed that the symbol was true, or that he had not been able to find further clues to the lost mine. *"I know one thing, kid,"* Jerry Black had said cryptically. *"If you ever find that old derrotero your great-grandfather made, you just might get a lead on the Lost Espectro."*

Gary rolled the *derrotero* within the photograph and replaced them in his pack. He started down the slope to the floor of the gloomy canyon. Lobo stood still, then turned slowly and looked back along the way they had just traveled. He growled low and flattened his ears. The three explorers looked back. There was nothing to be seen. Lobo growled again.

Gary motioned to his two friends to take cover. He sank down behind a boulder and peered down the quiet canyon.

"What do you think it is?" hissed Tuck.

Gary wet his lips and felt for the field glasses. He focused them on the canyon and slowly swept every foot of it with the glasses. Nothing was to be seen, at least nothing that would threaten them.

"If that wasn't a rockfall that blocked us from getting back through that hole, and someone did block it, then mightn't they have waited until we left the cavern, then removed the blockage and followed us?" said Sue quietly.

Gary shrugged. He looked at Tuck. "You stay here with Sue and watch," he said. He handed Tuck his rifle and took the shotgun. "Don't do any wild shooting!"

Gary trudged down the slope, followed by Lobo. The dog kept looking back. Gary forced his way through a tangle of brush and then walked along-side the dry watercourse of the canyon. To either side, below the overhanging walls, were slopes of talus formed from the loose hanging rock that seemed ready to drop if one were to raise his voice in that echoing place. Thick and thorny brush had laced itself through the jumble. A snake would have had a hard time finding a way through the entanglements.

He rounded a curve and was a good half mile beyond the place where he had left his friends when the canyon widened. Here it was a mass of rock and brush through which the dry watercourse crept, almost turning completely back on itself at times. Sweat broke out on him as he forced his way through, grunting in pain as thorns pierced his clothing and flesh. He was finally forced to stop. He sat down on a flat rock and reached for his canteen. It was then that he saw the faint symbol carved into the opposite wall. He was on his feet in an instant, forcing his way across the tangle despite his weariness. He stopped on the treacherous slope below the symbol and stared at it. It was not familiar to him, although he lashed his flagging memory until his head ached. He then saw that the upper left and center part of the place where the symbol had been cut had flaked off through weathering. He half closed his eyes and then the realization came to him. The left-hand part of the symbol, as he faced it, should have been a reversed numeral 3, although in the case of this particular symbol they were not numerals, but rather brackets on each side of a word which was now incomplete. The complete symbol meant to stop and change direction.

Gary plunged down the slope, heedless of the thorny brush. He followed the rough bed of the old watercourse back along the canyon, studying each foot of the walls as he went along. He was almost back at the canyon junction before he knew it, and he had seen no further symbols.

Sue came down to him. "We haven't seen anything," she said.

"Forget about that!" said Gary. "Get Tuck!"

"Here," said the lean one as he came toward them. He eyed Gary. "You look excited, *amigo*. You see Asesino?"

Gary told them of his find. "We'll have to work to the other end of this canyon for more clues."

"What about *him?*" asked Tuck, jerking a thumb over his shoulder toward the canyon through which they had just traveled.

Gary whistled sharply for Lobo. He pointed to the narrow canyon. "Go, boy," he said. The dog trotted up the slope and vanished in the brush.

"No one will get past him," added Gary. "At least he'll let us know if anyone is around."

Gary led the way. They had walked a quarter of a mile when they turned a bend to find themselves looking at a thoroughly blocked canyon, filled with masses of rock and earth. There was no way under, around, through, or over that blockage.

"Crazy," said Tuck. "From what I figure, the canyon of the arrastres must be somewhere beyond that blockage. No wonder we couldn't find a way from there into here."

Sue was poking about with a stick. "Hey," she said. She picked up a rusted mule shoe, one of the type with the flared ends. "I wish this thing could talk."

"We'll have to work back," said Gary.

Slowly and carefully they scanned the walls until they reached the place where the narrow canyon joined the one they were in. Lobo dozed on a rock. "Well," said Gary, "that shows he didn't find anyone."

"Or whoever was in there went back," said Tuck.

They all looked at each other. The threat from the unknown was being far overshadowed by the thoughts that the mine must be somewhere close to them. "*¡Adelante!*" said Gary.

More than an hour passed. It was Tuck who

made the next discovery, a rather curious symbol on a flat rock, almost completely covered by brush and a litter of gravel. The symbol was a stylized snake with the head pointing across to the western side of the canyon. There wasn't any doubt that the rock upon which it had been carved had been in that particular position a long time. They crossed the dry watercourse, for the symbol was plain enough. "Treasure on opposite side," it seemed to hiss.

The western side was a terrible jumble of rock with labyrinthine passages, some of them thoroughly choked with brush, weaving through the mass. The three of them examined every open rock face, then began to poke through the brush to examine others. Time drifted past and there were no new discoveries. Nothing but naked rock and cruel brush.

Tuck climbed a sloping rock ledge, then jumped down on the far side. There was a crashing sound and the hoarse voice of Tuck mouthing imprecations.

Gary grinned. He walked up the slope and looked down. All he could see was Tuck's head, the rest of his body was concealed by the ever-present brush.

"Anything down there?" asked Gary.

Tuck was still muttering. "Nothing but black dirt," he growled.

"Black dirt? In there?"

Tuck held up his hands. They were mottled black. "Well anyway, it's charcoal or something," he said.

Gary dropped on his belly. "Kick around a bit," he said.

Tuck's head vanished. In a few minutes it appeared like the head of a busy gopher. "Charcoal, all right," he said. "Seems like someone had a big fire in here."

"Gary!" called Sue from the other side of the ledge. "There's another hole here and the bottom is black too. Charcoal, I think."

"Eureka!" said Gary. His eyes widened.

"You loco or something?" asked Tuck.

"Charcoal, you dope! Charcoal pits were used by the old Spanish and Mexican miners to heat their drills so they could temper them! Man, we're close! We're *so* close!"

"There's another charcoal pit over here," said Sue. She paused. "Something else too! Another one of those snakes! Pointing right up this slope, Gary!" She popped out of the hole and pointed up the almost impassable slope toward the masses of rock clogging the western side of the canyon.

"We're almost right on top of it," said Gary in a hushed voice. "Up the slope! ¡*Adelante!*"

They wasted no time, tired as they were, for the fever was now upon them—the treasure-hunting fever that begins slowly and then steadily and ever increasingly takes over the mind and the body until it reaches the raging heat that sometimes consumes those who harbor the insidious disease.

"There's one of those crazy mule shoes," said Sue, pointing to a symbol carved on a squat boulder.

Gary looked at it. It did look like a mule shoe except for the three dots within the shoe. "It's not a mule shoe," he said slowly and quietly. That symbol means a flight of steps, indicating that the treasure is down in a shaft or a cave."

"But *where?*" said Sue. She looked at the wild and forbidding area about them and then dropped her hands helplessly by her sides.

"Fifty *varas* away," said Gary in a faraway voice. He walked to the upper end of the squat boulder and pointed to an odd-looking symbol carved there.

"*Varas?*" questioned Sue.

"A *vara* is thirty-three and one-third inches," said Gary.

"Which way?" asked Sue.

"Will that help?" said Tuck. He pointed beyond the boulder to yet another symbol, a horizontal cross. The long part of the upright pointed directly up the slope.

"About forty-six paces," said Sue, "figuring on a three-foot pace, or thereabouts. There should be something else in that area to show us the rest of the way."

"How confident she is," said Tuck.

Gary began his pacing, but it was almost impossible to keep to a standard pace because of the terrain. When he reached the end of his pacing he stood in an area where openings of all sizes and shapes, some of them in the ground, others against the side of the canyon, showed like the unseeing eyes of the blind. There must have been at least two dozen of them.

In and out of the holes they popped like busy ground squirrels, but found nothing to indicate that the holes were anything but works of nature. Gary looked along the slope. "There are other holes along there," he said wearily.

"Too far from the symbol," said Sue.

Gary nodded. He shoved back his hat. He leaned back against a flat slab of rock upon which Tuck Browne stood like a gaunt statue eying the jumbled slope. The flat slab was almost against the canyon wall. Tuck moved his feet. Gary's mouth dropped open. He leaned forward and shoved Tuck's left foot over. "Say!" said the lean one. His jaw dropped too as he saw Gary pointing to a carved sign where Tuck had been standing. "Treasure in a tunnel, *directly beneath this sign,*" said Gary.

An intense, brooding quiet seemed to shroud the canyon. Then the faint, far-off muttering of thunder sounded over it.

12 The Lost Espectro

GARY GOT DOWN on his knees and examined the thick slab of rock supposedly resting atop a tunnel which held the treasure that had been lost for so long. It would take powerful modern equipment to move the slab, yet it had either been placed there above the tunnel about a hundred years ago, or the tunnel had been dug *beneath* it. Gary reached for his pack and took out his light, folding entrenching tool. He pulled loose rock aside and then began to probe into the hardened earth beneath the slab.

"Chow time," said Sue laconically. She placed the food on the slab.

Gary nodded absentmindedly. Tuck came up the slope and dumped a load of driftwood near the slab. "I picked out the strongest of the stuff for shoring, Gary," he said. He shook his head. "I still don't like the idea of digging down under that slab."

"How else do you expect to get into the tunnel?" snapped Gary. His nerves were getting edgy.

"We could go back outside and get help," said Tuck.

Gary stubbornly shook his head. "We've got to find out what is under here first, Tuck, before we go and make fools out of ourselves."

"He's right, Tuck," said Sue.

They ate quickly and with little talk. Now and then they could hear the far-off rumbling of thunder high over the darkening Espectros. The canyon was a gloomy, forbidding place at any time, but now with the darkening sky it was positively frightening. A cold wind swept through it now and then, thrashing through the brush and moaning around the bends.

Gary finished his meal and set to work again driving a shallow hole beneath the edge of the slab. Tuck and Sue looked at each other over

Gary's head. Now that they had reached their goal they were feeling somewhat let down; both of them had expected to walk into a neatly shored drift and find piles of gold ingots covered with dust, ready for the taking. Now they did not know how long it would take to find out just how true those symbols atop the rock slab might be. The noise of the thunder, and the wind, and the utter loneliness and isolation of the place had begun to prey on their nerves. Yet neither of them had the courage to tell Gary what they thought. Gary was stubborn, and he was determined to get beneath that slab. Meanwhile, the sands of time were running steadily and a little too swiftly to suit the Brownes. Darkness would trap them in the canyon if Gary did not agree to leave soon.

He was on his belly now, driving the tool deep beneath the slab. Despite the coolness of the air he was dripping sweat, and his hands had begun to redden with forming blisters from the hard work.

Tuck shrugged at Sue. "Let me take over, Gary," he said.

"I'm doing all right," said Gary.

"Two of us taking turns can dig faster than one alone."

Gary looked up. He wiped the sweat from his

dirty face. "The quicker we find out, the quicker we can leave, eh?" he said a little sarcastically.

Tuck picked up the tool. "Take it easy," he said quietly. "No use getting gold fever."

"Sure," agreed Sue. "Like in the books where one man goes loco and kills off the others once they find the gold. You know, in that picture we saw one time. I . . ." Her voice trailed off as she saw the look on Gary's dirty face. "Heh, heh," she said. "Well I better do the dishes, fellas, being as how I am *cocinera.* Heh . . ." She began to gather the food supplies and to repack them in Tuck's haversack.

"See if you can find a water hole," said Gary shortly. "Don't go too far!"

"I'll be all right," she said. "Besides, Lobo is down the slope. He won't let anyone bother me."

Tuck was digging steadily. He looked back at Gary. "You think this slab might cave in?"

"Most of it seems to be resting solidly."

"Yeh, well I don't want it resting solidly on *me.*"

Gary walked around the slab and examined the ground between it and the cliff face. He took the other entrenching tool and began to dig. Here the earth seemed softer, and in no time at all he was down several feet. He threw off his hat and shirt and began to dig steadily.

Tuck stood up and wiped the sweat from his face. "Well, that was a waste of time," he said. "Struck solid rock down there."

"Give me a hand!"

The two of them made the earth fly until they were waist-deep in the hole. Gary crawled out to get his canteen, for it was hot, dry work. He drank and then started toward the hole to give Tuck the canteen. He stopped as though he had run into a stone wall when the terrified scream came from the canyon below him. He dropped the canteen and snatched up his rifle. He ran down to the place where he had last seen Sue, for it was her voice that was awakening the echoes. Then she appeared, legging it up the slope as hard as she could go. Gary ran down to meet her with ready rifle. She staggered a little. "Don't go down there!" she gasped. She reached Gary and gripped his arm. "I saw somebody down there!"

Gary crouched behind a rock ledge and motioned her to do the same. He eyed the lower canyon. There was no sign of life down there. "Did you see who it was?" he asked.

She swallowed hard. "All I really saw was a head. I had found water in a hole and was just bending down to see if it was good enough to use when I had the oddest feeling I was being watched. I looked up and there he was—about fifty yards from me, on the other side of the dry watercourse, staring right at me, Gary. I got scared, I tell you! I opened my mouth to yell and nothing came out."

"That was a switch," said Gary dryly.

"Funnee, oh funnee! Well, I got my voice back, and when I screamed he vanished. Poof! just like that!"

Gary eyed the far side of the canyon. It was almost impossible to distinguish things because of the gloom. "You sure you didn't see who it was?" There was no answer from the girl. "Sue?" he added. He turned.

"It was his eyes," she said shakily. "Gary, I'll swear it must have been Asesino!"

His blood ran cold. Despite himself he shivered a little. "Cut it out!" he said.

"No," she insisted. "He wasn't wearing a hat, Gary, just a band of cloth about his thick dark hair like you see in the pictures of the old-time Apaches."

"He's just a legend now," he said firmly.

"No one knows for sure if he is dead," Sue said quietly.

Lobo came quietly up the slope. Gary eyed the big dog. It was strange that he had not made some commotion. "Lobo didn't seem to see or hear anything," he said.

"Can a dog *see* or *hear* a *ghost*," she said in a low voice.

"That's loco!" he said. "Let's get back to Tuck."

She walked up the slope ahead of him. Gary looked down at Lobo. "Didn't *you* see anything?" he asked.

Lobo looked back at his master. There was no trace of excitement about the dog. Gary shook his head and walked up the slope. Now and then he looked back down toward the floor of the dark canyon. There was nothing to be seen, yet he, too, felt as though he were being watched.

"Tuck!" called Gary.

There was no answer from the lean one, and no sound of metal striking earth.

"Tuck!" called Gary again.

There was no sound from Tuck. Sue looked quickly at Gary. A veil seemed to pass over the canyon as a cloud drifted high overhead; the canyon now had a twilight gloom about it.

"Tuck?" called Sue.

Gary looked down the slope again. It was as deserted as a lunar landscape. He walked around the rock slab; there was no sign of Tuck. A cold feeling came over Gary. Supposing, somehow,

Asesino had gotten up *behind* Gary and Sue, and had spirited away Tuck? It was really impossible for a being of flesh and blood to do it, but then Lobo had not seen or heard anything. His heart skipped a beat. "Tuck?" he called.

Nothing; not a sight or a sound of the lean one. The hole was empty. The slope showed no signs of Tuck. Gary peered about; he was downright frightened now. He almost wished he had listened to the others and had left while they had had a chance to leave. "Lobo," said Gary. The dog sniffed up and stopped beside him. "Go find Tuck, Lobo."

Lobo padded off through the brush. He stopped at a clump of thick and tangled brush that was matted against the rock wall. He looked back at Gary.

"Go on, Lobo!" said Gary. "Find Tuck!"

Lobo stood stock-still. He whined a little.

Gary walked to the dog and stared at the brush. He looked down at Lobo. "Find Tuck," he repeated angrily.

Lobo whined and poked his nose into the brush. Gary pulled some of it aside, and a cool draft played about him. Suddenly his hair seemed to stand on end, for a ghostly, faint voice was calling his name. "Gary! Oh, Gary! Gary!"

Gary shivered. The voice seemed to come from the brush itself. He pulled more of it to one side and the cold draft grew more pronounced. Then he plainly heard the voice beyond him and much lower than he was. "Gary! Oh, Gary!"

He started forward. Lobo barked sharply. Gary's left foot began to sink and he jumped back, slipping and falling heavily. Gravel rushed from where he had been standing and pattered hollowly down below somewhere.

"Thanks, *amigo!*" came the strangled, hollow-sounding voice. "Whyn't you dump down that rock slab while you're at it?"

Gary got down on his hands and knees and worked his way back into the brush. His right hand struck a rounded edge of earth and then probed into nothingness. He bellied forward and found an irregular hole close beside the rock face. The cold air played about him as it rose from the black depths. "Tuck?" he called. His voice echoed below.

"Yeh, it's me," answered Tuck "Black as ink down here. I got tired of digging. Saw a rabbit run into that brush. Thought it might taste good if we needed more food. All of a sudden I found myself falling and I landed down here."

Gary closed his eyes. Green sickness welled

up within him and his throat tasted sour. Many a man had been lost forever by fooling around just such old mine shafts and caves.

Sue came up behind Gary. "Where is he?" she asked.

"Don't come any closer," warned Gary. "He's all right."

"I got lonesome out there," she said.

Gary got the packs, tools, rifle, and shotgun and brought them to the place where Tuck had dropped from the face of the earth. There were two coils of light nylon rope in the packs. He took one of them and fastened a bull's-eye lantern to it. "Line and lamp coming down, Tuck," he said. He lowered away.

He could see the lantern light alternately illuminating each side of the deep hole as it swung about. Then he saw Tuck's dirty, frightened face in the yellow pool of light, only to lose it again. He lowered the light a little more and it swung about to light something else, something white and bony—a human skeleton complete with grinning, hollow-eyed skull. Then it, too, was lost from sight as the lantern spun about once more. Tuck's shriek blasted against Gary's ears. Gary had the presence of mind to whip the end of the nylon rope quickly around a shattered tree stump that was near the edge of the brush. The rope tightened, and feet scrabbled against the sides of the shaft. Tuck's harsh and erratic breathing echoed hollowly. In record time his head popped up out of the opening. Gary grabbed him and dragged him out on the ground. Tuck lay there shivering with fright, taking in air with great gulps.

Gary gathered his courage and looked down in the hole once more. The lamp twisted and again lighted the human relics. Shreds of rotted clothing hung on the pitiful framework, and one bony hand rested on what seemed to be a book. It was then that Gary noticed the thick tree trunk to one side of the hole; it had deep notches cut into it. His heart leaped. It was a sure-enough Spanish miner's chicken ladder!

Tuck gasped. "It wasn't that skeleton that bothered me, *amigo,* it was the bad air down there."

"Sure, sure," said Gary soothingly. He looked back at Tuck. "I think you literally stumbled into the Lost Espectro, Tuck."

"You sure?"

"No, but I soon will be."

"You going down there?"

Gary nodded. "It isn't the skeleton I'm afraid of,

Tuck, it's what Sue saw down in the canyon." He told Tuck of Sue's experience.

"Who do you think it was?" asked Tuck after a long pause.

"*Quien sabe?* The dog didn't see or hear anything."

"You think she might be kidding us?"

"I am not!" said Sue angrily from the background.

Gary looked up at the dark sky. "It's getting late," he said. "We can't possibly get out of here tonight. I say we stay here. Hole up in one of those caves. Two of us stay on guard all night. Lobo won't let anyone get near us without a warning."

"Sure," said Sue sarcastically "He sure gave us a warning about that somebody down there, whoever it was."

"Maybe he knew who it was," said Tuck thoughtfully. "Someone *he* wouldn't be concerned about. How would he know about our suspicions about certain people?"

"You might have something there," said Gary.

"Whoever it was, sure looked like an Apache," said Sue. "How many Apaches does Lobo know?"

"Jerry Black?" said Tuck.

Gary shook his head. "I don't know if he ever

saw Jerry," he said. He looked at the two of them. "Maybe someone is *playing* Apache."

"Fine time to be playing cowboys and Indians," growled Tuck.

"That's not exactly what I meant," said Gary. He picked up his rifle and checked it. "A white man can have dark hair and bind it with a cloth like Apaches used to do. *Someone whom Lobo knows . . .*"

"I'm scared," said Sue. There was a catch in her voice.

"Look, Sue," said Gary, not unkindly, "we're stuck in here. If anyone is looking for trouble we're better off to staying right where we are and letting them come to us than trying to get out of here in the dark. We don't know any way out of here other than the way we came in, and it would be pitch black in there before we ever reached the cavern. We can't take a chance of trying to find another way out of here, if there *is* such a thing."

"Besides, Susie," said Tuck bravely, "we've found the Lost Espectro. We can't just go off and leave it here, can we now?"

"How do we know it's the Lost Espectro?" she demanded.

"There's one way to find out," said Tuck with a

brave and careless smile. He seemed to grow a little in height. "Go on down there and make sure."

"Bravo," said Sue.

Tuck turned. "Don't you worry about a thing, Gary," he said. "I'll keep good watch up *here* while you're down *there* making certain it is the Lost Espectro."

"I might have known," said Gary dryly. "O.K. I didn't come all the way into this hole in the mountains to turn away from the Lost Espectro at the last minute." He handed Tuck the rifle, put on his shirt, and picked up his hat. Gary formed a sling for the shotgun from a length of rope and slung it over his back. Then he took the second coil of nylon rope and slung it over his arm. He lowered his legs into the shaft and felt for the first rungs of the chicken ladder, holding onto the rope that he had dropped for Tuck. Gary tested the ladder all the way down and found it solid, preserved from rot by the dry air of the shaft.

He detached the lantern from the rope and flashed it about. Behind the sprawled skeleton was the dark, irregular opening of a drift. He flashed the light on the skeleton. It had been there a good many years. He knelt and examined the clothing. It was so old that some of it crumbled in his grasp, releasing a little cloud of musty dust that swirled about in the lamplight and then rose up into the shaft. An eerie feeling as well as the ancient dust seemed to float about Gary. He gently removed the leather-bound book from beneath the bony fingers and opened it. It was a Spanish Bible. A nameplate showed in the yellow light, and written upon it in a spidery script was a name. "Leandro Melgosa," read Gary quietly. He looked at the skeleton. According to history, Leandro Melgosa had been the youngest of the three Melgosa Brothers. Vigil Melgosa, the second brother, had been killed by Apaches, while Marcos, the eldest, supposedly after hiding the mine, had fled to Mexico and had never returned. Nothing had been known of the fate of Leandro. He had vanished in the Espectros like the snows of yesteryear.

Gary stood up. He stepped over the skeleton, and as he did so a queer, sickening feeling of cold horror came over him. He could see the back of the skull, *and in it was a large and ragged hole.* Someone had evidently killed Leandro, if indeed it *was* Leandro, from behind, unless of course he had fallen and fatally struck himself. Gary reached out a trembling hand to touch the hole. As he did so the skull fell to one side. Something rattled on the floor of the shaft. Gary knelt and picked up a mutilated lead slug. He had been killed by human hands then.

Thoughts of the other killings in the Espectros flooded through his mind. *Killings in which men had been shot through the back of the skull!* He was confused. No one murderer could have spanned the long years from the time of the killing of Leandro Melgosa up until twelve years or so ago when the two prospectors, John Bellina and Carl Schuster, had been shot to death through the back of the head. There was an eerie puzzle here. He stepped over the skeleton and raised his lamp. The rays picked out sketchy carving on the drift wall. "*Dios Mio, ayudame,*" read Gary. He wrinkled his brow. "My God, help me," he translated. Farther down a deep cross had been cut into the rock and beneath that was more writing. "There is nothing but death in this canyon," he translated. There was a signature beneath the last word. "Marcos Melgosa, August 17, 1844," he added slowly.

There were mystery and hidden tragedy in those words. Gary flashed the light up the drift. Here and there on the floor were pieces of wood which had fallen from the sagging pit props supporting the narrow tunnel. Amidst the litter were woven baskets. Gary recognized them as *mecapals,* used by the Spanish and Mexican miners to carry ore from mines. There was also a pile of sotol stalks, once used by the old-timers as torches.

He raised the lamp and shot the light down the drift. It had not been cut straight as American miners would have done—driving in a drift, then crosscutting to get at the vein—but in the old Mexican method of following the vein itself and not removing any more earth and rock than was absolutely necessary.

Something held Gary back. The prospect of walking alone up that twisted, dark, and echoing drift was not too inviting. He stepped back, hesitated, then walked forward again along the drift. What puzzled him was the steady current of fresh air flowing about him. It indicated only one thing —there was another opening to the mine somewhere in the bowels of the rock ahead of him.

He saw a worn-out husk sandal on the floor and a rawhide *zurrón* bag that had once been fastened to the head of the man who had carried ore in the *zurrón* from the mine. On and on he went, his boots crunching in the debris fallen from the roof and walls of the drift, watching carefully for holes or weak spots in the packed earth of the drift bottom. The draft still blew about him, but there was no sign of a gold vein in the walls, or any caches of the precious metal that had been left behind so long ago.

The place was too much for his nerves at last. There was a brooding, haunting air about the drift. He turned to go back, and instantly it seemed to him as though something had moved up close behind him out of the fearsome darkness to reach out bony claws for him. He almost panicked. Then he began to count each step to himself. He had taken thirty paces into the drift. He held off gibbering panic and at last reached the shaft. Gary forced himself to stand there; disciplining himself. "Tuck!" he called.

Sue thrust her head into the hole. "What is it, Gary?"

"I haven't found much of anything," said Gary. His voice cracked a little.

"You want Tuck to go back with you?"

She knew all right. She knew Gary was fighting for self-control down in that drafty dark hole in the ground. Sue smiled. "Maybe Tuck ought to stay on guard," she said. "I'll go with you, Gary."

He swallowed hard. "It's all right," he said. He knew she was as scared as he was. The kid had guts all right. Scared as she was, she didn't want him to go in there alone again. She came lightly down the ladder. She eyed the skeleton. "Who was he?" she asked.

Gary shrugged. "Leandro Melgosa as far as I know. The brother that vanished."

She gingerly walked past the skeleton. "Seems to me his brothers should have buried him."

"Vigil was killed by Apaches. Marcos returned to Mexico." Gary looked down at the remains of Leandro. "I think he was murdered right here, Sue."

She smiled wanly. "Why?"

"Someone shot him through the back of the head." Gary's eyes narrowed. He flashed the light on the writing. "I wonder," he said quietly.

Sue was an A student in Spanish. She quickly translated the inscription. "My God, help me! There is nothing but death in this canyon. Marcos Melgosa, August 17, 1844." She looked at Gary. "He was just frightened, that's all, Gary. His other brother had been killed by the Apaches; then Leandro was killed, and Marcos knew he had to get out of here or die as well. He didn't have time to bury Leandro."

"But he had time to cut that inscription into the rock," said Gary quietly. He looked down at the skeleton. "He didn't even take the time to lay out his brother properly. Just let him drop there in death right across the drift entrance."

There was a puzzled look on Sue's face. "So?"

"Maybe Marcos left Leandro as the *patrón*."

"So what? A *patrón* is an owner, an employer, Gary. Maybe Marcos . . ." Her voice trailed off. "How could a dead man be an owner or an employer?"

Gary felt a creeping horror within him. "There is another meaning to the word *patrón*, Sue. The old Spanish miners would sometimes take as much gold or silver from a mine as they needed, or could carry at the time, then to guard the mine they would kill one of the peons or Indian slaves so that he would be a *patrón*—a ghostly warden or guard of the mine to keep out intruders."

"But Leandro was his brother!"

"Yes. But Marcos had gold fever. He knew he had to leave the mine, and there was no *patrón* to place on guard. *No one but his own brother.*"

Sue shuddered. "Now we know why he never came back here again. Imagine coming down here to see Leandro still on guard!"

"I saw him," said Gary dryly. "So did Tuck. I don't think we'll be bothered by the ghost of Leandro Melgosa. I have a feeling his ghost was waiting for one man alone. Maybe the ghost, if there is such a thing as a ghost, left here and went to look for Brother Marcos. *That* would have been a meeting!"

Now that Sue was with him, Gary felt his courage return. If a girl had the nerve to come down into that dark mine he could hardly back out now from further exploration.

"Maybe there is nothing in the mine," said Sue.

"Then why would Leandro have been left behind as *patrón*?"

"That's true," she said. "Won't hurt to look. It doesn't seem to be much darker or any more dangerous down here than it is up there."

Gary smiled at her, then turned to lead the way back along the dark and echoing drift. A stone struck the bottom of the shaft. A moment later Tuck whistled softly. "Gary," he croaked in a low voice. "There's someone coming up here!"

Gary shook his head at Sue, then swiftly ascended the ladder, crawling on his belly through the brush to lie beside his partner. He raised his head and caught a swift and furtive movement amidst the tangle of rocks and brush. The canyon was very dark now and the wind was getting colder. Gary flipped off the safety on the shotgun. Tuck raised the Winchester and full-cocked it.

Minutes ticked past. There was no further sign of life. Gary's eyes ached from peering into the gloom. He raised his head a little higher, then some strange intuition made him quickly turn his head to the left. A man was standing behind a shattered boulder with only his head and shoulders showing; his thick hair was bound with a cloth, exactly as Sue had described the stranger.

Gary threw up his shotgun and Tuck turned, raising the rifle. Gary sighted and then his breath caught in his throat. The man stood up in plain view and smiled widely. He waved a hand. "It's Lije Purtis, fellas," he said. There was no sign of a weapon on him.

"Come out in the open," said Gary coldly. "What do you want?"

Lije shambled out into the open and smiled again. "I wanted to tell you someone has been following you. You got anything to eat?"

"Yes," said Tuck. "Who is following us, Lije?"

Lije shook his head as though to clear it. "I followed him through that cave way back there, at the water hole. I was goin' to ask him for some . . ." The rifle cracked flatly from a hundred yards down the slope. Lije fell heavily. The echo of the shot slammed back and forth in the canyon as the boys dropped flat. Gary crawled to the edge of the rocks in front of him, and just as he did so lightning flashed high in the heavens. The eerie light played full on the gaunt face of Lije Purtis. His mouth gaped open, revealing his yellow teeth. His eyes stared at the dark sky, but they did not see. They would never see anything on earth again.

13 Trapped

THE CANYON WAS QUIET AGAIN except for the moaning of the wind. The acrid odor of burnt powder drifted away. Nothing had been seen of the hidden marksman except the quick, stabbing spurt of flame from his rifle muzzle. His accuracy had been remarkable at that distance, firing uphill and in the uncertain light. If he had done nothing else, he had at least cleared poor Lije Purtis of any suspicion—not that it would help Lije now.

Gary passed the shotgun to Tuck and took the rifle. Tuck was a good shot but not in a class with

Gary. There was no use in fooling themselves. The chips were down and it might soon be a question of kill or be killed. Strangely enough to Gary, there was almost a feeling of relief within him as he peered through the shifting light. He had become tired of the unknown and the unseen. He knew now it was no ghost that haunted the Espectros. It was a man of flesh and blood, armed with a heavy-caliber rifle, who thought nothing of killing. Lije Purtis had known who he was; therefore Lije had died. It was as simple as that.

This time Gary would shoot to kill rather than fire warning shots as he had done at the shadowy figure who had been watching for them that moonlit night in the canyon of the water hole.

Lobo rounded a huge slab of rock and dropped to the ground beside Gary. Gary looked curiously at the dog. If it had been Lije Purtis whom Sue had seen, it was logical enough that Lobo wouldn't have barked at *him*. Lobo knew Lije and knew he was harmless. What puzzled Gary was the fact that Lobo was so calm now. Had he seen the man who had killed Lije? *Did he know that man as well as he had known Lije?* Was that why he was so unconcerned?

Tuck was evidently puzzled as well. He looked down at Lobo and then up at Gary, shrugging his shoulders. Gary worked his way over to Tuck. "What do you think?" he asked.

"*Quien sabe?* Lobo must know who it is. Someone *he* thinks is all right."

"That's what I'm thinking. On the other hand, if it was Asesino, he wouldn't stay any longer in one spot than it takes to fire a shot. He's too slick for that, Tuck."

Thunder rumbled in the sky. A few cold drops of rain pattered quickly on the rocks. Gary eyed the position they were in. The mine was just below them, probing beneath the sheer cliff behind them. To the right and the left the cliff walls curved down toward the floor of the canyon. Before them was the tangled slope covered with shattered rock from which the killer had fired. If he were still on that slope he could easily see anyone trying to make the floor of the canyon. When full darkness came he could move in, taking his chances on the fact that Lobo knew him. He could wait through the darkness of the night, watching and listening for any movement, and when the light of dawn flooded the canyon, he could pick his position so that he could see a fly crawling across those rocks near the mine.

Gary took stock. They had enough water for another day or so and enough food for about the same amount of time—with short rations, of course. Gary had a full magazine in his rifle and about a dozen extra cartridges, totaling twenty rounds; Tuck, with the short-range shotgun, had only half a dozen cartridges. At close range the shotgun was a deadly weapon, but if the unseen marksman stayed away from it he would be safe enough.

The wind shifted and carried another sound with it—a thin, mocking laugh that came from up high. Gary raised his rifle, but he decided there would be no sense in shooting at the elusive voice. Maybe that was what the killer wanted; the quick, spurting of fire from the Winchester would enable him to pinpoint Gary. The way he could shoot, he'd hardly need more than that.

Tuck paled. He crouched lower, and his knuckles whitened as he gripped the shotgun. He looked toward the sound of the voice, and even as he did so the swift red-orange spurt of flame etched itself high on the canyon wall to the right. The slug splattered itself on the rock a yard above the two boys as the echo of the shot tumbled in raucous confusion down the canyon.

"Get down," said Gary. He jumped up and then dropped. The rifle flashed again. This time Gary saw the darkness of a man behind the flash of the rifle, and he fired twice. He knew instantly that he had fallen victim to the instinctive bad habit of firing too low when shooting upward.

The mocking laughter came again from a different place. There was an eerie, haunting quality about it, as though it came from the lips of a madman.

Gary lay low. The quick sight he had had of the man had been long enough for him to see that the man did not wear a hat. He remembered the old saying of years ago in Arizona in reference to fighting Apaches. "Shoot 'em if they don't wear a hat!" It was a fair rule of thumb.

"Asesino?" queried Tuck hoarsely.

"I don't know."

"Who else could it be?"

They were interrupted by a shaky little voice emanating from the shaft behind them. "I'm scared down here," said Sue.

"I'm scared up here," said Tuck.

Darkness was swiftly filling the canyon. The thought of lying there in the open in the coming darkness with a madman stalking them was a frightening one. Ten minutes passed. Something struck the rocks ten feet in front of them and shattered, scattering shards of broken rock through the air like grenade fragments. A moment later another rock plummeted down and crashed five feet to one side of Tuck. He grunted in pain as a bit of the rock slashed across the back of his right hand. The laughter floated across the canyon and echoed back so that no one could say where it came from, so confusing were the echoes. The laughter was followed by the crashing impact of more rocks.

"Get into the shaft," said Gary quickly.

"We'll be trapped," said Tuck.

"You want your skull smashed! We haven't any choice!"

Tuck scuttled down the ladder. Gary backed up against the rock wall. He pulled up the nylon rope and tied it about Lobo, then lowered the heavy dog into the shaft. It was too dark to see anything now. Swiftly he lowered their gear down into the hole. He looked up at the dark rim of the canyon and saw someone flit past, then vanish. "Who are you?" he yelled. "What do you want?" The echoes fled down the canyon. "*Who are you? Who are you? Who are you? What do you want? What do you want? What do you want?*" They died away to be replaced by the moaning of the dusk wind.

There was no answer. Gary glanced once more toward the still form of poor Lije Purtis. His last words came back to Gary. "I followed him through that cave way back there, at the water hole. I was goin' to ask him for some . . ." What had he wanted from the unknown?

The voice came clearly from the darkness, now to the left. "Asesino . . . Asesino . . . Asesino . . ." It was followed by that eerie, mocking laughter slowly dying away.

Gary wasted no time, He clambered down the chicken ladder, with the strong premonition that it wasn't quite the thing to do; they might be trapped in there forever. But there was no choice. He was confused and he could not think clearly. "Get back into the drift," he said.

The three of them stood there in the pool of light from the bull's-eye lamp. The draft played about them. Gary looked along the dark drift. "The draft means there must be an opening somewhere along there," he said.

"Somewhere," echoed Tuck. He swallowed hard.

"It's a chance we have to take," said Gary.

Tuck looked upward. "Maybe he knows where the opening is. Maybe he'll be waiting there for us."

"Cut it!" snapped Gary. "We've got guns! We can shoot too! We're not licked yet!"

"Hear! Hear!" said Sue.

Something pattered on the floor of the shaft.

Gary flashed the lamp that way. Silvery drops of rain showed in the yellow light. Faintly and insistently the muttering of thunder came to them.

"Well anyway, we're out of the rain," cracked Tuck. He subsided immediately when he saw the looks shot at him.

"Keep guard here, Tuck," said Gary. "I'm going to explore this drift." He walked to the pile of sotol stalks he had seen and gathered some of them, returning to Tuck to give him the lamp. He lighted one of the sotol stalks and started down the tunnel, followed by Lobo. "Go back," he said. He went on alone, following the winding passage, holding the flaring stalk high. His footsteps echoed on the hard, dusty floor of the drift. Now and then he had to squeeze under dangerous places where the props had sagged; at other times he had to clamber over piles of rock and earth that had fallen from the sides and top of the drift. It was reassuring to feel the constant draft blowing about him. The air was a little musty, but it was fresh enough to indicate that it came from the outside, no matter how far it was up the drift.

Here and there were the dark and narrow entrances to crosscuttings. Some of them had been filled by earth and rock when the props collapsed. Some of them were not very deep. The old miners had followed the winding of the vein, scooping out the rich ore wherever it was. So far he had seen nothing of the ore itself, for they had been thorough enough in their digging. He wasn't much interested at this point in the legendary tales of the wealth of the Lost Espectro, if this was indeed the Lost Espectro. He knew now that life was more precious than finding the treasure reputed to be buried in the old mine. Lead fever had replaced gold fever; the lead from Asesino's rifle.

The flickering light revealed a roughly squared-off room cut into the drift. Suddenly, Gary realized he had just enough of the sotol stalks to light his way back to the shaft. He peered into the room, saw that there was a further continuation of the drift on the opposite side, then turned back. He did not want to have to traverse any of the distance back in the darkness.

The last stalk flickered out as he turned the last bend in the drift before reaching the shaft. The light went out and he was in complete darkness. He should have been able to see the light from the lamp by now. He hesitated as he stared into the blackness, feeling sweat from his perspiring hands beginning to grease the stock of his rifle. Supposing something had happened to his two friends? Supposing he was now alone in that drift? *Supposing somebody was waiting for him in the blackness after disposing of Sue and Tuck?*

He tried to call out but his mouth was as dry as ashes. Then he whistled softly. Something pattered on the floor of the tunnel and he heard Lobo's welcoming bark. "Tuck?" called Gary softly.

"Quiet!" said the lean one from the blackness.

Gary felt his way along until he touched Tuck. "What is it?"

"We thought we heard someone up there."

Gary cocked his head to listen. The rain was still pattering down and some of the drops fell into the shaft. He was about to chide Tuck for a false alarm when he heard the scuffling of feet at the top of the shaft. He stepped back into the drift and raised the shotgun. Gravel dropped into the shaft. A moment later the eerie, mocking laughter came to them. There was a haunting madness to it.

This time Lobo sensed something. He barked savagely and then growled deep in his throat. Gary held him back as more gravel tumbled into the shaft. If that unknown made a move to reach the chicken ladder he would meet the full blast of both shotgun barrels. And even Asesino couldn't evade that.

There was a scuffling noise and something heavy dropped at the top of the shaft. Gary reached for Tuck and took the lamp from his hands. The scuffling noise came again. This time Gary chanced a light, flicking it up the shaft in time to see a heavy tree trunk fall across the opening and the quick withdrawal of a wet hand. He saw, with a sickening conclusion, that there were several other timbers already in place across the narrow opening. He flicked out the light as gravel tumbled down toward him.

Cold sweat trickled down Gary's sides. The madman was blocking them in as he had blocked the dry entrance to the cavern far back in the canyon of the water hole. "What do you want?" yelled Gary. "Tell us! *What do you want?*" His voice seemed to boom in the shaft.

"Gold," said a faraway-sounding voice. "The gold . . ."

"We haven't found any!"

Gravel trickled down again. The scuffling continued. Gary chanced another lighting of the lamp. This time he clearly saw the wet face peering down between two of the logs. The dark hair, bound by a dirty wet cloth, and painted across the nose were two bands of white paint, while the dark eyes seemed to burn with madness and hate. Then the face vanished and the eerie laughter drifted down to them again.

Gary stepped back. His hands were shaking. Tuck gripped him around the shoulders. "Who was it?"

Gary shivered. "It was him all right. Asesino. I saw him, Tuck. *I saw him!*" Gary's voice rose sharply.

Tuck's hand cracked against Gary's head. "Snap out of it, *amigo!*" he said. "Don't *you* go loco on us! We need you, Gary! You can't let us down now!"

Gary's nerves calmed down. "Thanks," he said quietly. "Never thought I'd be thanking a fella for bopping me."

Gary walked back into the drift. They could hear their attacker hard at work up there, blocking the way. It would have been better to have hunted for him, as he had hunted for them. But with a man like that, an outlaw hunted for so many years, his senses would have been honed to the edge native only to animals.

"He said he only wanted the gold," said Sue.

"He said he wanted gold, and there wasn't any *only* in what he said," corrected Tuck. "In the first place, we haven't got any gold. In the second place, if we did have it, and we let him have it, do you think he'd let us get out of here alive?"

Lobo was now almost in a paroxysm of rage. He barked and growled, and the sound of it was a terrible thing. Gary finally managed to quiet him. There was no sound coming from above. Gary aimed the light up the shaft again. All he could see were the logs, with packed dirt and rock showing between them. They had been neatly sealed into the shaft, and there wasn't any doubt in Gary's mind about who was waiting up there for them if they tried to dig their way to freedom.

Gary lighted the lamp again when he was in the drift. "Come on," he said. "There's air coming in here from somewhere. We've got food and water. We're not licked yet!"

Tuck grinned. "I never thought I'd have to belt you, Gary, but now that I did, I'm not sorry. *¡Adelante!*"

Gary led the way back to the large squared-off room and into the drift beyond it. Ten minutes later the three of them stopped in dismay. The drift had narrowed and a heavy fall of rock had almost completely sealed the passageway. Air drifted through the narrow space between the top of the drift and the piled-up debris. Gary crawled up the pile and flashed the lamp over it. The air blew damply against his face, but he could see little with the lamp. They'd have to dig through.

The three of them set to work, with Sue relieving the boys in turn, while Lobo stood guard behind them. Now that the entrance to the shaft had been sealed behind them, the draft died away and the stifling dust hung heavily in the drift, but the air was fresh enough.

Gary was ten feet into the pile when Sue crawled up beside him. "Maybe we ought to rest," she suggested wearily.

Gary shook his head. "No," he said. "We keep on!"

"It's after eleven o'clock, Gary!" she protested.

Gary jerked a thumb back over his shoulder. "He isn't sleeping," he said quietly. She knew whom he meant.

Hours passed, and then Tuck weakly drove his entrenching tool against a big rock. The handle snapped and then the rock slid heavily down a steep slope, followed by Tuck riding the slide to the bottom of the drift. Gary crawled after him and flashed the weakening lamp up the drift. The way seemed clear enough now. The two of them crawled through their little tunnel to get Sue. She was sound asleep with her back against a pit prop and with Lobo's head nestled on her lap.

Gary walked partway back into the drift to listen. It was as quiet as the grave. He winced mentally at the simile. That squared-off room had been puzzling him all night. He walked slowly back to it and flicked out his lamp to replace the batteries. He lighted the lamp again and instantly saw a niche cut into the far wall with something resting upon it.

"Come on, Gary!" called Tuck. "The bus is leaving!"

"Wait a bit!"

The two Brownes came into the room. Gary walked toward the niche and flashed the lamp upon the shelf. His breath caught in his throat. There were half a dozen objects resting upon it, somewhat brick-shaped, but about half the size of a common brick, and the edges were roughly rounded. Dust was thick upon them. He reached out a hand and then quickly withdrew it, stepping back to flash the light on the roughly hewn wall.

"What is it, Gary?" asked Tuck.

Gary turned slowly. "I think we have found what we've been looking for," he said quietly.

"A way out?"

"No. Gold, *amigo!*"

"Those bricks?"

Gary nodded.

"Let's get 'em and get out then!" Tuck started forward.

"Wait!" snapped Gary.

Tuck turned slowly. "Why? You loco?"

Gary shook his head. "We've got to watch for traps." He picked up his entrenching tool and firmly lashed it to the barrels of the shotgun. He raised the gun, then jerked his head at the two Brownes. "Get back into the drift," he cautioned. He reached forward, slid the edge of the tool beneath an end brick, and lifted it up. He turned and passed it back to Tuck. Again he reached out and scooped up another brick, passing it back to Tuck. Sweat appeared on his brow as he lifted the third one. Nothing happened. He was almost ready to grab the rest of them by hand, but something held him back. He scooped up the fourth brick and as it cleared the shelf, something creaked dryly.

"These are *pure gold!*" said Tuck wildly.

"Gold!" shrieked Sue. "Gold!" She danced madly about. "Get the rest of 'em! *GOLD!*"

Gary began to lift the fifth brick, and as he did so the creaking noise came again, but this time it was louder. He dropped the brick and jumped back. As he did so Tuck flashed the light on the wall. The wall was moving, falling forward with a creaking, grating noise. Then it fell heavily and solidly, some of the material striking Gary's feet. The wall was completely collapsed, and the rays of the lamp reflected dully off piles of the roughly shaped bricks set into the hewn-out area behind the wall. Then the roof dropped to conceal the amassed wealth of the Lost Espectro. Gary slammed full tilt into Tuck and Sue, driving them along the drift as rock and earth thudded behind them, raising a thick, choking cloud of dust. "Run!" yelled Gary. He turned to look back. Tuck flashed the lamp and through the thickening dust they could see a bizarre sight. A lean wet face, streaked with white paint, peered through the swirling haze, then the mouth opened to shriek madly.

Gary raised the shotgun and wildly fired both barrels, not even bothering about the lashed entrenching tool that thrust itself out from the barrels like a spade bayonet of ancient times. The noise from the gun was deafening. The face vanished behind the dust and more falling rock and earth. Gary did not stop to see the result of his firing. He was running for dear life along the drift, with rock and dirt pattering down behind him. He saw Tuck's legs wriggling out of sight atop the tunnel block and he dived in after them. Tuck broke into the open and slid wildly down the slope, with Gary helter-skelter, head over heels, atop his partner and Lobo atop Gary.

Gary handed the shotgun to Tuck and took the rifle. The three of them had their gear slung about them. It was no time to be choosy. There was one way to go. They slogged on along the echoing drift, spurred on by their fear.

Twice more they had to clear their way through blockages, but they were nothing as compared to the big one far behind them. The drift sloped upward and the draft became stronger; a wet, freshening smell replaced the dusty odor of the drift.

Gary rounded a sharp turn in the tunnel and saw a steep slope. He scrambled up it. They had been climbing steadily almost since the time they had left the gold cache. Water was trickling along the side of the drift now and he could have sworn he heard the faint rumbling of thunder. He rounded yet another turn and found himself in another large room. At the far side was a tattered sheet of cloth waving in the strong breeze that blew into the room. He started toward it, then stopped short. An odd, eerie feeling came over him. Tuck and Sue came into the room, puffing and blowing.

Gary turned slowly and swung the lamp. To one side was a crude bunk and in the bunk was a hunched figure, covered with a filthy blanket. One arm hung over the side of the bunk, and the hand that rested on the floor was nothing but drawn, parchmentlike skin that clearly showed the bones.

"What is it?" said Sue weakly. "Not *again*, Gary!"

"He's long dead," said Tuck. "The *dead ones* don't bother me any more."

Gary's feet grated on rusted tin cans as he walked toward the bunk. He slowly and steadily pulled back the blanket to look into a mummified face framed by thick, coarse black hair. The mummy had been there a long, long time, preserved by cool dry air. A dingy headband bound the hair to the head. Gary stepped back. His feet struck tin cans again. He flashed the light down on them. Some of the labels were still legible. "Elberta peaches," he said quietly. He raised the lamp. A Winchester rifle leaned against the wall, covered with a patina of rust and dust. Gary walked to it and picked it up. He knew enough about guns to recognize a Model 1886. He worked the stiff action and ejected a heavy brass cartridge. He picked it up and looked at the base of it. "A .50/110 caliber," he said. Gary looked at his two friends. "I think we've found Asesino. He's been dead many years."

Sue shivered in the draft. The wind whipped the tattered cloth at the room entrance and moaned down the drift.

"If that's Asesino, and I don't know who else it could be," said Tuck quietly, "*who was that back there?*"

Gary leaned the heavy rifle against the wall, flicked out the lamp, and walked to the curtain. He pulled it to one side and stepped out onto a rock shelf with a rough and almost natural-looking breastwork of rocks along the outer edge. For a moment he expected to be looking down the canyon of The Needle. Instead he saw the thick grayness of the false dawn and far below, a canyon. For a moment he was confused, until he realized it was the very canyon in which the entrance to the Lost Espectro was. From where he stood he could easily see anyone who moved on the slopes or in the canyon. Even now he saw a stealthy movement. Someone was skulking along the edge of the canyon. Someone with a heavy rifle in his hands and a dirty cloth bound about his dark wet hair. He was looking down toward where the entrance to the mine should be.

Gary stepped back into the room. He lighted the lamp, knowing well enough the man outside could not see the light. "Our little friend is out there," he said, eying his two partners closely, "looking down toward the mine entrance. Maybe he figures we just might dig ourselves out that way. He knows now we found the gold. What do we do? Sit it out here? Try to make a break to get away? Or clean his clock for him?"

Tuck grinned. "You think I'm leaving here without taking a crack at him? After the way he scared me? No, sir!"

Sue spit inelegantly into her left palm and smacked it with her small right fist. "Let me at him," she growled fiercely. Lobo began to growl, too, as he started for the entrance.

Gary flicked off the lamp. "Quiet, Lobo," he said. "Stay! Our boy probably won't look back this way. That's a break for us. If we get close enough we can get the drop on him."

"Supposing he doesn't surrender?" said Sue anxiously.

There was a long moment of quietness.

Sue spoke again. "Now that was a stupid question, wasn't it?"

The rain pattered down steadily and the wind whined through the canyon as the three of them made their plan.

14 End of a Killer

THE RAIN WAS DRUMMING on the Espectros, streaming from a real buster of a cloud that hung over the mountains. The cloud was a huge and threatening mass with a distended belly of gray and black which held a mighty tonnage of water. The Espectros had long been notorious as the breeding place of storms, and when the Thunder People rumbled their great drums in the deep canyons and lanced the streaming skies with their shafts of lightning tipped with flashing death, it was no place for frail man to stand up against nature. The wind bellowed through the gorges and lashed the scrub trees. Water had begun to course through the dry stream beds at the bottoms of the canyons, rising with frightful speed and sweeping everything before its fluid power.

Gary Cole knew it had been pouring rain for most of the night while he and his companions were burrowing in the belly of the Lost Espectro. There had been other rainstorms of more than average intensity over the Espectros that summer, but he could not recall any as fierce as this one. It was almost like dusk in the canyon country as he peered from behind the breastwork to spot the killer who haunted the canyon rim. Then he saw a movement in a clump of brush at the very edge of the chasm. "Ready?" he asked over his shoulder.

"Hold it a minute," hissed Tuck from within the cavern. "I'm not finished with my makeup!"

Gary turned to look at Sue and his heart went out to her. Her great brown eyes looked like those of a frightened doe as she hunched back against the rock face out of the driving rain, holding onto Lobo's collar. "Remember, Sue," he said quietly, "I want you to release him only if things turn against us."

She nodded. "I'll remember," she said.

Gary looked at the shotgun beside her. "It's loaded. I showed you how to throw off the safety catch. Don't fire both barrels at the same time! If anything happens to Tuck and me, lay low. He might not find you. If he gets too close let the dog go at him, then use the gun."

She closed her eyes, swallowed hard, then nodded again.

Gary crawled around the edge of the tumble-down breastwork and bellied down the slope behind a screen of wet rock. In no time at all he was wet to the skin, but it didn't matter. The hunt he was on and the tension of it was enough to keep his mind from his discomfort. He was halfway down the slope when he looked back. Tuck's head popped up. The lean one waved, then vanished again. Gary gave him time to get into position, then crawled on.

The killer was well hidden in the tangled brush that covered one side of a huge tilted slab of rock at the very brink of the canyon. Gary could just make out the outline of his prone figure. Gary inched along, cradling his Winchester in the crook of his arms, until he reached a place to one side of the slab of rock where the ground was a little higher. He was no more than thirty yards from his quarry.

He waited again, feeling the cold rain beating

steadily against his back. Minutes ticked past and then he saw a furtive movement to his right, beyond the slab of rock. Tuck was in position now with Asesino's old rifle.

Gary bellied down the harsh wet slope. Then he stopped short, for there had been a movement in the tangle of brush. He saw two boots protruding from beneath it. They were small boots and the heel on the left one had been set crookedly in place. The sight laid nerve-chill upon rain-chill. It was too far away to distinguish the double crescent of nails set into the crooked heel, but as sure as his name was Gary Cole, he knew that the crescent was there.

The rain slackened a bit. Gary picked up a fist-sized rock and threw it over the brink. He hardly heard the sound of it striking far below, but the killer heard it. He must have hearing like a dog. As he moved, Gary saw the wet dark hair, bound with the dingy cloth, but the man's painted face was turned away from Gary as he peered intently down into the canyon.

Gary moved closer. He eased the hammer of his Winchester back to full cock. It would be an easy shot. He could hit the killer and he'd never know what had hit him. But it wasn't in Gary to kill that way. An intense curiosity came over him. Gary wanted the man to turn his face so that he could see it plainly, for his other views of it had been too short to know who he was. Maybe he would not know the man at all.

Gary shifted to raise his rifle, and the metal-shod stock struck a rock. The effect of the noise was instantaneous on the killer. He turned and was on his feet, crouching flat against the rock. As he raised his rifle he was looking directly at Gary. It was no one Gary recognized.

Higher on the slope a heavy rifle crashed. The killer's eyes widened. He looked past Gary and his mouth squared like that of a Greek tragedy mask. He was trying to yell or cry out. Gary turned to see a tall, gaunt figure striding down the slope—a figure wearing ragged clothing, with long black hair bound by a dingy cloth and bands of white paint drawn across his nose and upper cheeks. A heavy Winchester was in his hands and as he came down the slope he gave forth with a piercing, wailing cry that seemed to congeal Gary's blood.

"Asesino!" screamed the killer at last.

"Throw down that gun!" yelled Gary.

The man turned to stare at Gary. Gary ran forward. The rifle came up and the stock struck

Gary on the shoulder. He dropped his own rifle and then ducked under another blow of the rifle, staring into the wild, dark-blue eyes of the killer. "Tuck!" screamed Gary. He jumped to one side and saw the disguised Tuck fall headlong over a rock, his rifle clattering down the slope.

It was no time for niceties. Gary kicked the killer in the belly, and as he came down with his head in a reflex action, Gary rammed his right knee up to meet the down-coming chin. The man grunted in pain. He staggered to one side and fired his rifle. The blast of flame and smoke half-blinded Gary. He threw his hands over his face and fell backward against the rock slab as the killer levered another round into the smoking rifle. A lean figure hurtled down the slope. The rifle roared and Tuck hit the ground an instant ahead of the bullet, but the stock struck his head and kept him down there.

The killer jumped back to reload his rifle. Gary could hardly see him. At this moment a dark shape came roaring into battle—it was Lobo. The dog rose cleanly from the ground and struck savagely at the killer. The man fell backward. His feet clawed for a hold on the crumbling brink of the canyon, then with a wild, piercing scream he went down. There was a thudding noise just below the rim of the canyon, then the distant clattering of the rifle as it struck far below.

Thunder roared in the canyons and lighting etched itself across the dark sky to lance into a distant peak. Gary rubbed his eyes and then crawled to the edge of the canyon to look down. Twenty feet below him was a narrow ledge, and lying flat on the ledge was the killer with his wide dark eyes staring right back at Gary, but they could see nothing. Gary rubbed his eyes again. The man's hair was no longer thick and black, but rather thin and blond. Just above his head lay a rain-soaked black wig.

Tuck bellied alongside Gary. He stared too. "The *Candyman,*" he said in an awed voice.

Gary nodded. He began to feel his intense weariness, the pain in his shoulder, and the bitter coldness of the lashing rain. "You played a great part, Tuck," he said. He gripped his partner's shoulder.

"It was your idea, Gary."

Gary stood up. "It was too close to suit me."

From somewhere up the canyon came a subdued roaring that gained intensity as they listened. Then it seemed as though the canyon was filled with a towering wall of gray and white. It was water—a great mass of drainage water trapped in the narrow canyon and raging along through it to seek an exit. It leaped from side to side like some insensate and blinded primeval beast, as it battered at the walls, carrying within its swirling liquid belly tons of rock, brush, shattered trees, and anything else it could gobble down, using the rough mass to scour the bottom of the canyon like some gigantic sanding machine.

It was a mad orgy of sound; a world of insane water and crackling lightning underscored by the rumbling of the thunder. From high on the canyon rim came silvery streams of rainwater to add to the flash flood. The water swirled with incredible speed up the slope below the cliff upon which the boys were standing in wide-eyed awe. It swept against the cliff base, rising higher and higher until it seemed as though it might even lap around the feet of the two watchers, then slowly, ever so slowly, it began to subside. The swirling surface was stippled with drowned animals, tangled mats of thorny brush, and splintered trees.

Despite the danger and the cold rain they could not leave until the flood began to recede. Farther along the canyon the crest still roared and raged.

Gary dropped to his belly and stared down at the base of the cliff as the water trickled off. Where the great rock that marked the site of the Lost Espectro had been was now a smooth area of gravel and sand, overlaying the original rocky slope. Even as he watched, great masses of rock fell from the cliff face and shattered on the slope. There was no way he could locate the shaft now. Perhaps it was lost forever. No one could ever trace it without the cryptic symbols left by the Mexicans over a hundred years ago.

They did what they had to do. They got the nylon ropes, and Gary let himself down the crumbling ledge where the Candyman lay. They hoisted the body and placed it beneath the rock slab, covering it with rock to keep the coyotes from it. They did not look back as they returned to Sue. Despite the pouring rain, none of them wanted to take shelter in Asesino's cave.

They packed their gear. Now they had only three gold bricks since one had been left behind somewhere along the winding drift. But nothing in the world could have made them go back after it. Even the gold they had saved didn't mean much to them. They wanted, above all, to get away from the dripping mountains of violent death.

They were south, a good mile away from Asesino's cave, on the rugged mesa top when the lightning struck with fearful intensity against the bald rock face high above the concealed cave entrance, the back door to the Lost Espectro. Slowly at first and then with gathering power, a great side of rock and rain-loosened earth cascaded smoothly down the slopes until the once rough facing was a smooth mass of rock and mud at rest, with Asesino entombed, perhaps forever, beneath the great new covering.

They did not look back again as they picked their way down a crumbled cliff into a wide canyon, which Gary recognized as the lower part of the canyon where the water hole that had been formed by the great landslide of years past was located. Three horsemen urged their mounts toward them, and the worn-out trio recognized Sheriff Larry Gray, Jim Kermit, and the dark smiling face of Jerry Black.

Jim Kermit shook his head as he unscrewed the top of his big Thermos and began to pour coffee for them. "You kids had everyone worried sick," he said. "My Francie found out Sue had left the house, and she called me at Millerton to tell me about it. I found the jeep you left behind and got in touch with the Sheriff here. Luckily Jerry Black was in making his monthly report to the Sheriff, so he came along. Believe you me, kids, you had everyone scared to death. Mrs. Kermit called Tucson and got in touch with your mother, Gary. She's on her way home. Your pa is all right. I also called *your* pa and ma, Tuck."

"Thanks, oh thanks," murmured the lean one.

Sheriff Gray looked at Sue. "I have a rough idea who is going to get the worst of this thing," he said with a sly grin.

"Yeh," said Sue. "Jolly, isn't it? Heh! Heh!"

Gary looked at Jerry Black. "Monthly report?" he said questioningly.

Jerry nodded. "The state assigned me as a special investigating agent to see if I could get any ideas as to who was killing people in the Espectros. That's why I pretended to be writing a book while I stayed at the old Mills place. It gave me an excuse to look about in those mountains. Frankly, I didn't believe much in those killings, but I liked the freedom the job gave me except when I was keeping an eye on you two characters."

"What do you mean?" asked Tuck.

Jerry grinned. "Oh, I was watching you. It wasn't easy because of that dog. He seemed to know a real Apache was prowling about. The only time I really got worried was the night you boys were coming out of this canyon and Gary took a couple of potshots at me."

"So that was you!" said Gary. "You nearly scared us to death!"

"How do you think I felt when you shot at me?" said Jerry. "Kid, you shot as fast and as accurately as any combat Marine I ever knew."

"I wasn't trying to hit you," said Gary. "Just scare you off."

"You did that!"

"Did you ever really suspect anyone?" asked Sue.

Jerry shook his head. "I had no leads at all. Of course I knew there were all kinds of oddball characters poking about those mountains. I had nothing on any of them."

"Did you ever suspect Fred Platt?" asked Gary.

"Him?" Jerry threw back his head and laughed. "The Candyman is scared to death of those mountains. He is the last person I'd ever suspect."

"That's rich," said Jim Kermit with a grin. "The Candyman! Hawww!"

The sheriff shook his head. "You kids," he said with a smile.

"Tell 'em, Tuck," said Gary.

The lean one emptied his coffee cup. He *told 'em*, complete with histrionic gestures and intonations that would have put a Barrymore to utter shame. At the conclusion of his harrowing tale, Sue took out the three gold ingots and handed them to the sheriff. He hefted them and whistled softly. "You say there are a lot more of 'em in that mine?"

"Enough to make all of us richer than Croesus," said Sue offhandedly. She casually inspected her dirty and broken fingernails. "Maybe buried forever, of course," she added.

"Incredible," said the lawman.

They took the three worn-out kids up behind them and rode to the jeep. Gary got the motor started on the third try.

Jerry leaned on his saddle horn and eyed Gary. "Did you know there were a number of rewards posted for the murderer?" he asked.

"No," said Gary. He was sick of talking about the Candyman.

"Amounts to somewhere between three and four thousand dollars as far as I can recollect. *Dead or alive*, Gary."

"We can guide you back to the body, Jerry,"

said Gary. "But I'd rather not talk about it now."

"I understand."

Gary drove to the graveled road and then along it toward the main highway. Tuck spoke when they were on the pavement. "Well, we found out the truth about Asesino *and* the Lost Espectro. I wonder what Fred Platt thought when he saw me coming down that slope. Must have been quite a jolt."

"It was," said Gary. "Enough of a jolt to kill him off. The Candyman! When I think of those four days I rode in the same truck with him, shooting off my mouth about my theories on the Lost Espectro and all the clues I had, it makes me pretty weak inside, I tell you."

"He must have spent a lot of time in those mountains," said Sue, "without even a good lead on the Lost Espectro until *we* showed him the way."

"Poor Lije," said Tuck. "All he probably wanted was a can of Elberta peaches from the Candyman. It was his death sentence. They'll never find Lije's body now."

"Maybe that's the way he wanted it," said Gary quietly.

"There will be more ghosts in the Espectros tonight," said Sue. Suddenly she shivered.

"As far as I'm concerned," said Gary, "they can have the Espectros. I've had my fill of them."

"Me too," said Sue fervently.

A gentle and melodious snoring came from the lean one, seemingly echoed by the low growling of thunder over the rain-misted Espectros.

15 A Person Without a Dream Is Dead

GARY COLE CAME OUT OF THE SHOP with his mother's Christmas gift tucked under his arm. The cold December wind swept down from the Espectros and moaned through the lamplighted streets of Cottonwood Wells. Gary looked up and down the street for Tuck and his Honda. The lean one was standing at the nearest corner beside his motorcycle talking to a girl. Gary walked toward them. It would be a good Christmas for the Coles. What with the reward money and the money from the gold they had taken from the Lost Espectro, the Coles were making plans for the dude ranch Pete had always wanted.

Gary eyed the girl as he came up behind Tuck. She was a doll, tall, dark-haired, and well dressed. "Hey, *amigo*," he said. "Introduce me!"

Tuck turned slowly. "You loco, man? Remember our partner when we hunted the Lost Espectro? The one who got shipped off to boarding school in Phoenix to keep her from fooling around the Espectros?"

Gary stared at her. Gone were the ugly braces and the generous sprinkling of freckles. Gone was the short-cropped and untidy hairdo. Gone were the Levi's and the faded checkered shirt, the battered old hat, and the dusty boots. Susan Alice Browne was no longer the hoyden who had helped solve the mystery of the Espectros. She was now a young lady.

"Close your mouth, Gary," she said gently. "You look much better that way." She smiled. "I was allowed home for Christmas."

"You make it sound like a reform school," said Tuck.

Gary swallowed. "How is it, Sue?" he asked.

She raised her head a little. "I must say the atmosphere is more congenial and *much, much* more *polished* than that of Cottonwood Wells Union High."

"Yeh," said Tuck. "Lookit her, Gary!"

Gary actually felt embarrassed. The metamorphosis of Susan Browne from lowly caterpillar into lovely butterfly was almost impossible to believe.

Tuck grinned. "Gary doesn't have a date yet for the Christmas dance, Sue."

She smiled gently. "A *kid* dance? Rock and roll no less!"

Gary eyed her and the devil took over. "Well, Sue, I'd be happy to take you, but I'm not sure I want to go myself. Jerry Black thinks he has a good lead on a couple of burroloads of silver that were buried near Massacre Spring about seventy years ago, and since we have Christmas vacation now, Tuck and I figured we'd take a crack at looking for it. So we have to get our plans made and our gear ready. Sorry about the dance. Good night, Sue." He started to walk toward his jeep.

"Gary Cole!" she snapped. "So happens I *do* want to go to that dance with you! So happens *I* have a Christmas vacation *too!* And if you think for one minute that you and my cousin Tucker C. Browne are going to look for that silver without *me*, you have another think coming!"

Tuck rolled up his eyes. "Now you've done it, Gary," he said. "Can't trust you one minute."

The three experienced treasure hunters started out through the cold night air toward the Cole ranch, Sue Browne riding beside Gary in the jeep, and Tucker C. Browne leading the way on his roaring Honda, trying to cut down his time between The Wells and the ranch. To the northeast bulked the dark and brooding Espectros, still holding many of their old secrets and perhaps some new ones as well. They held a spell over those who had been born in their shadows, a spell that could never be broken in a lifetime. For if the Espectros had not given the trio of treasure hunters great riches, at least they had given them a place to hunt for them, and a person without a dream is dead.